camp CONFIDENTIAL

grace's Twist

GROSSET & DUNLAP
Published by the Penguin Group
Penguin Group (USA) Inc., 375 Hudson Street, New York, New York 10014, U.S.A.
Penguin Group (Canada), 90 Eglinton Avenue East, Suite 700, Toronto, Ontario, Canada
M4P 2Y3 (a division of Pearson Penguin Canada Inc.)
Penguin Books Ltd, 80 Strand, London WC2R 0RL, England
Penguin Ireland, 25 St Stephen's Green, Dublin 2, Ireland
(a division of Penguin Books Ltd)
Penguin Group (Australia), 250 Camberwell Road, Camberwell, Victoria 3124, Australia
(a division of Pearson Australia Group Pty Ltd)
Penguin Books India Pvt Ltd, 11 Community Centre, Panchsheel Park,
New Delhi - 110 017, India
Penguin Group (NZ), Cnr Airborne and Rosedale Roads, Albany, Auckland 1310,
New Zealand (a division of Pearson New Zealand Ltd)
Penguin Books (South Africa) (Pty) Ltd, 24 Sturdee Avenue, Rosebank, Johannesburg
2196, South Africa

Penguin Books Ltd, Registered Offices:
80 Strand, London WC2R 0RL, England

This edition published in 2006 by Grosset & Dunlap, a division of Penguin Young Readers Group, 345 Hudson Street, New York, New York 10014. GROSSET & DUNLAP is a trademark of Penguin Group (USA) Inc. *PSS!* and *MAD LIBS* are registered trademarks of Penguin Group (USA) Inc.

Manufactured in China.

The Library of Congress has cataloged
Grace's Twist (ISBN 0-448-43875-5) as follows:
Library of Congress Control Number: 2004025128

This edition ISBN 0-448-44370-8   10 9 8 7 6 5 4 3 2 1

camp CONFIDENTIAL

Grace's Twist

by Melissa J. Morgan

Grosset & Dunlap

chapter

Dear Emily,

Hey there, chiquita! What's up back in Boringtown, U.S.A.? I bet you've been spending the whole summer just lying by the pool, right? I'm having a blast here at Camp Lakeview, as if that's any surprise! My bunkmates rule—they're almost as cool as you. (Calm down, I said <u>almost</u>!) I'm in the same bunk as Brynn, Jenna, and Alex again, which is so much fun. It's hard to believe I haven't seen them since last summer—we just slipped right back into our old friendship. I'm lucky to have so many friends here. Not that they'll ever replace you, my bestest friend in the world! I wish you could come to Lakeview, too. It's weird not seeing you for the entire summer. And I know you're probably mad at me. I'm sorry I haven't written yet, Em, but you know how it is. I keep meaning to, but then—

Whatever. I haven't told you the most amazing thing. One of the new girls in my bunk, Natalie, is the daughter of Tad Maxwell!! Can you believe it?? He came to Lakeview with his girlfriend once in the early days of camp, but he couldn't make it for Visiting Day last week. If only my parents were famous movie stars so they would be too busy to get here for a visit. But no, they showed up. With another boring book for me to read. Ugh. Can you believe it? Jenna's

*parents brought a truckload of food in their
care package, and my parents bring The
Jungle Book. Why would anyone want
to read that when they can just watch the
cartoon? Anyway, Mom and Dad spent the
whole time lecturing me, as I'm sure you can
imagine—*

Grace Matthews sighed and put down her pen. Her best friend, Emily, deserved a letter. She'd already sent three letters to Grace at Camp Lakeview, and Grace hadn't answered even one. But it took so long to write a letter . . . and there was always so much fun stuff to do at camp. Her copy of *The Call of the Wild* lay upside down at the foot of her bed, open to the last page she'd read. Grace grabbed it and pulled it halfheartedly onto her lap. Reading was almost as boring as writing. She glanced around bunk 3C at all her friends. Sure, some of them were reading or writing letters, but lots of them were busy doing more interesting stuff. Well, except for Chelsea, who seemed to be doing nothing but staring at herself in her hand mirror. Chelsea was beautiful, but it still had to be pretty boring to spend all your time looking at your own face. Grace shrugged and turned her attention to one of the other old-time campers like herself.

"Hey, Brynn," Grace called down from her top

bunk. "What on earth are you doing?"

Brynn stood in the center of the small room, her feet planted about ten inches apart on the scuffed wooden floor. She was bent over at the waist, her arms hanging down and her short dark red hair falling over her face. She'd been standing like that for at least two minutes. "It's yoga," Brynn said, her voice muffled. She was speaking into her knees, after all. "My mom gave me an article on Visiting Day about how lots of actors do yoga to keep themselves focused."

Grace grinned. She loved acting, and she knew Brynn did, too. In fact, it was the only real interest Brynn had. "Mind if I join you?"

Brynn shook her upside-down head. Grace jumped down from her bunk, took her place next to Brynn, and copied the strange position. Just before she bent over, she noticed Julie, their counselor, shoot a look up at the unfinished letter and book on Grace's bed. Grace felt her cheeks grow warm, and she quickly leaned over so she wouldn't have to meet Julie's gaze.

Hanging head-down wasn't much better, though. All the blood rushed to her head, making her cheeks and neck feel hot. Her curly red hair was longer than Brynn's, and it kept getting in her eyes and covering her face. She moved to pull away a strand that had gotten caught in her mouth, but Brynn protested. "You're supposed to keep still," she said. "Don't move; just pay attention to your breathing and to the stretch in your back muscles."

"That's right, Grace, don't forget to breathe," Jenna Bloom said from across the room. Jenna put on a slow, deep voice as if she were trying to hypnotize someone. "Breathe in . . . breathe out. Breathe in . . . breathe in some more," Jenna said in her "soothing" voice.

Grace couldn't help it—she got the giggles. "How can I pay attention to my breathing when I can't breathe?" she asked. Leaning over like this made it hard to take a deep breath, and she felt herself getting a little dizzy. She stood up quickly and got a head rush. "Whoa," she cried, stumbling backward. Luckily Marissa, bunk 3C's CIT, or counselor-in-training, was there to catch her.

"I'm not sure you're mellow enough to do yoga, Grace," Marissa joked.

Brynn stood up very slowly. "It's too bad," she commented. "You could be such a good actress if you tried. Yoga could really help you be more centered."

Grace decided to ignore her. Brynn's whole goal in life was to be a famous actor, and she could never understand why Grace wasn't as focused on that as she was. But to Grace, acting was just something fun to do. She loved it—she *totally* loved it—but mostly because it was easy, and she was good at it, and it gave her a chance to be someone else for a few minutes. She didn't need to be famous or anything. She just loved acting. Whenever things got tough in school, acting was her favorite way to escape from the pressure. But none of her bunkmates knew that. None of them had any idea how it was back at school. Summer camp was for fun, not stress, and that was exactly how Grace liked it.

"There's no more time for yoga now, anyway," Marissa said. "Dinner's ready. I just came back to grab my hair band—I forgot it." Marissa snatched a pink elastic band from her cot and took off, letting the screen door bang shut behind her as she scooped her long hair up into a ponytail. She and the other CITs were responsible for serving the meals in the mess hall. If you could call them meals.

"Okay, everyone, let's go chow down," Julie called.

"You don't have to tell me twice," Jenna joked, heading for the door. She was so athletic that she spent lots of time eating—she needed plenty of fuel to burn out on the soccer field. She, Alex, and Sarah were the big jocks in the bunk. Grace liked sports well enough, but she wasn't as obsessed with them as some of her friends.

"I think it's spaghetti night," Alex said. She rolled her eyes at Brynn, her best friend. "In other words . . ."

". . . cardboard strips in tomato soup," Brynn finished for her. They both laughed.

Grace had to admit, the food at Camp Lakeview wasn't gourmet. In fact, it was even worse than the cafeteria food back at school. But eating every night in the noisy mess hall surrounded by all the other Lakeview campers was enough fun that the food didn't matter.

She climbed down the two rickety steps from the cabin and followed her bunkmates along the path toward the mess hall. Natalie and Alyssa, another 3C camper, walked right behind her.

"I didn't even get to dance with him," Alyssa was saying. "It's no big deal."

"But he obviously likes you," Natalie replied.

Grace grinned and turned around to walk backward so she could talk to them. "Still talking about the camp social?" she asked. "It was almost a week ago!"

Alyssa shrugged, making her orange hair swing. She'd dyed it that color the night before the social—by accident. It was supposed to be red, but something had gone horribly wrong. Grace was secretly a little relieved not to be the most Ronald McDonald-like girl in the bunk for a change. But on Alyssa, the strange color actually looked good—sort of punk. Alyssa was so artsy that she could make anything weird seem stylish.

"Adam was totally flirting with Alyssa at the social," Natalie said. "And I know she likes him, too. She's just being shy."

Alyssa stuck out her tongue at Natalie. "And *you're* just trying to make us forget about you and Simon," she teased.

Grace laughed. It was true, Natalie's relationship with Simon had been the big topic of discussion in bunk 3C for the past few weeks. Well, first it had been Natalie's famous father, and then Natalie's sort-of boyfriend, Simon. But for the past few days, talk had been a little more serious in the bunk.

Grace glanced over her shoulder to see where Jenna was. She was tromping through the trees at the head of the group, as usual. "Hey, do you guys think Jenna's doing okay?" she asked, lowering her voice.

Natalie squinted at Jenna's back. "She's been kinda sticking to herself, I guess," she said. "But I think that's normal."

Alyssa nodded. "She's probably still embarrassed about the Great Animal Escape."

Grace shuddered just thinking about it. Jenna had always been a prankster—some of the best memories Grace had from the previous summer were of helping Jenna prank their rival bunk, 3A. But the night before this year's Visiting Day, Jenna had gone too far. She'd let all the animals from the nature shack out of their cages . . . and into the camp social. It had been mayhem, and Jenna had gotten in a lot of trouble.

"Adam says she'll be fine," Alyssa said. "And he should know, he's her twin!"

"Oh, is that what *Adam* says?" Grace joked.

Natalie laughed, but Alyssa didn't even blush. She could be pretty impressive sometimes. When Grace had first met her, she'd thought Alyssa was shy because she was so quiet. But in the past month, she'd discovered that Alyssa wasn't shy—she just didn't see the need to talk unless she had something to say.

"It must be nice to have a twin," Natalie commented. "It's like having your own built-in best friend for life."

"Yeah, must be nice," Grace agreed. She turned back around to walk forward. Suddenly Grace realized that her whole bunk was lined up in pairs. Jenna walked along chatting with Julie, whom she'd known for years because her whole family had been coming to Lakeview since forever. Then Brynn and Alex, Sarah and Valerie, Candace and Jessie, Alyssa and Nat . . . even Chelsea had a buddy. She was walking with Karen, one of the most timid girls in the bunk. That was sort of a weird combination, but the rest of the pairs were totally normal. They were all best friends. Everyone had a partner... except for Grace.

Grace felt a pang of homesickness. Well, maybe not *home*sickness, exactly. More like *friend*sickness. She missed Emily. They'd been best friends since kindergarten, and Emily knew everything about Grace's life and her family and all her issues . . .

Why don't I have a best friend at camp? Grace suddenly wondered. *Everyone else does.*

The thought had never occurred to her before, and it was so shocking that she stopped in her tracks. How had she managed to spend a whole summer here last year without making a best friend? And she'd been here for half the summer this year without one, too.

"Whoa, Grace, did you fall asleep standing up?" Natalie laughed, pushing her gently in the back. "I almost walked right into you!"

"Oh. Sorry," Grace mumbled. Nat and Alyssa stepped in front of her, and Grace trailed after them.

"It was nice to meet your mom on Visiting Day," Alyssa told Natalie. "She's more my speed than your father. No offense."

"Don't worry. Even I can't keep up with my dad's crazy life," Natalie replied. "But I always have fun with my mother. And she really liked your parents—she told me so."

"Yeah, maybe over the winter we can all hang out," Alyssa said. "Our parents can keep one another busy, and then we can get away with doing whatever we want!"

Natalie grinned and gave her a high five.

Grace sighed. If only her parents were the kind of people she could have fun with. But they never even seemed to understand the idea of fun. Lately the only thing they did was give her lectures or "talks" or "suggestions." Even at Visiting Day, they hadn't wanted to talk about camp. They'd wanted to give her another lecture.

Snap out of it, Grace ordered herself. *Mom and Dad aren't here now. So I don't have to think about it.* She was here at Lakeview, her favorite place in the world, and she was going to enjoy every minute of it. Or at least she was going to try. It would be easier, though, if she could talk to someone about what was going on . . .

Grace quickened her pace, catching up to Natalie and Alyssa. They were still talking about Visiting Day, but Grace's mind wasn't on their conversation. She just watched the two of them, walking along close together, teasing and laughing with each other . . . they'd only known each other for a month, and yet they acted like old friends. Best friends.

I can't believe I didn't finish that letter to Emily, Grace thought, horrified. What if her best friend really was mad at her for not writing all summer? Grace had promised and promised that this year would be different. That this summer she'd actually keep in touch. The whole time, she'd known that Emily didn't believe her. Emily assumed that she wouldn't get a single letter from Grace, and so far, she was right.

Grace took a deep breath. Of course Emily wouldn't be mad. Emily understood how hard it was for Grace to write . . . that it took too long and kept her from relaxing and having fun at camp. Emily would just shake her head and laugh, because that's what best friends did.

A burst of laughter erupted from Natalie and Alyssa in front of her, and Grace felt a little flicker of jealousy. If she had a best friend at camp, she wouldn't have to keep this all to herself. She'd be able to talk about her parents' annoying behavior at Visiting Day. She'd be able to talk about . . .

Oh, never mind, Grace thought. *I have lots of friends here. And that's better than just one. Isn't it?*

chapter

TWO

"Whoo-hoo!" Grace yelled the next day on the path from bunk 3C. "Time for drama!" She pumped her arm in the air like a demented football fan.

Alex giggled, but Brynn rolled her eyes. "It's time for drama, Grace, not time to be *over*dramatic."

Grace stopped pumping her arm and instead draped it over Brynn's shoulders. "Okay, I'm just playing around," she admitted. "But I *am* psyched for drama. It's my favorite free choice."

Alex pushed back a branch that stuck out into the path, then held it so it wouldn't hit Grace and Brynn. "Then why didn't you take drama last session?" she asked Grace.

Grace shrugged. "Everybody likes drama. I figured I'd give some of the other kids a chance. And besides, I did put it as my number three choice last session. Julie just didn't give it to me."

"She always gives me drama for my free choice," Brynn said. "She knows there's no way I'd be cooped up with the smelly animals in the nature shack when I could be honing my craft."

"Phoning your what?" Grace teased.

Brynn laughed. "That's what my mother calls it. 'Honing my craft.' I think it means rehearsing."

"Wow. All that practicing *and* big, new words. I'm impressed," Grace said.

"What's your other free choice, Grace?" Alex asked.

"Arts and crafts."

Alex wrinkled her nose. "Yuck, I hate arts and crafts. The clay smells so bad."

"Maybe I'll do an improv scene about that in drama," Grace joked. "I'll pretend to be throwing a pot on the wheel, and then I'll act as if I'm overcome by fumes." She staggered backward, pretending to gasp for air.

"Very convincing." Alex giggled. "You'll definitely get a role in the camp play."

A little thrill of excitement ran down Grace's body. It was true, she wasn't as consumed by drama as Brynn. But that didn't keep her from being psyched by the idea of the play. "Now *that* would be fun," she said. "I wonder what play they're doing this year."

"*Peter Pan,*" Brynn said. "I'm so excited!" She nudged Grace in the side. "And remember, we have unfinished business from last summer."

"Oh. That's right. I forgot." Grace tried to sound casual, but inside she felt a rush of humiliation. She'd been hoping Brynn wouldn't remember their deal.

"What unfinished business?" Alex asked.

"Grace and I made a pact at the end of last summer," Brynn explained. "She was so mad at herself for not auditioning for the camp play last year that we promised we'd audition together this year—and that we'd both get parts!"

Grace kept a smile plastered on her face. Now was not the time to tell Brynn that she might not be able to keep up her end of the bargain. *Maybe I can audition,* Grace thought. *Maybe.*

"I can't believe you made a pact and you didn't tell me," Alex teased Brynn.

"I don't have to tell you everything," Brynn said.

"Yes you do. That's what best friends do." Alex playfully rolled her eyes. "Tell her, Grace."

"It's true. Best friends tell each other everything," Grace confirmed. She thought about Emily. Emily was the only one who knew what was going on in Grace's life right now. If only she were here . . .

"Okay, I broke the best-friend rule," Brynn said. "Can you ever forgive me?"

"Sure. That's also what best friends do. But don't let it happen again!" Alex joked. "Here we are."

They stopped in front of the dilapidated cabin that housed the drama department. Grace knew from last summer that the place was bigger inside than it looked from outside. The whole cabin was one big, open room, painted black, and the only furniture were black wooden boxes that acted as chairs, tables, couches, and whatever else was needed. All it took was a little imagination to make the place feel like a palace or a diner or a store in the Wild West. That's what made drama class so much fun.

"Uh-oh," Alex murmured, stepping closer to Brynn and Grace. "Looks like you're in for trouble." She pointed with her chin toward a tall, skinny girl just entering the drama shack.

"Oh, no," Brynn said. "A spy from bunk 3A!"

They all laughed. Their bunk had an old rivalry

with bunk 3A. Grace wasn't sure how it had started—when she arrived at camp last summer, one of the first things she learned was that 3A was the enemy. It didn't really matter why. The play rivalry was just for fun, anyway. Last week the girls from 3A had jokingly sprinkled food coloring on 3C's fried chicken at lunch. They hadn't noticed it on the food, but by the time they finished eating, Grace and her entire bunk had bright orange coloring on their fingers and lips. Not even swimming in the lake had gotten the color off their hands. So the 3A girls probably figured that 3C was planning some kind of prank as payback.

Alex and Brynn sneered at the 3A girl as she walked inside, then cracked up.

"We'll just have to *act* like we don't mind her," Grace joked.

"Have fun!" Alex gave her friends a little wave and headed off toward the newspaper shack for her own free choice.

Grace followed Brynn into the cool darkness of the drama shack, her heart beating fast with anticipation. "I can't wait to hear about the play," she told Brynn as they sat on the floor with the kids who were already there. "I mean, being on the stage crew was a lot of fun last summer, but I'd rather at least be one of the background actors."

"Yeah, that was pretty cool," Brynn replied. In last year's play, she had been one of the youngest kids onstage, even though she didn't get to say any lines. "If you don't goof around this year, you can get a part, too," she added.

Grace didn't answer. Brynn was right—she'd been so busy clowning around during drama last summer that she hadn't even managed to memorize the lines for her audition scene. But she'd learned her lesson. That was the reason she'd made the pact with Brynn—so that she'd be serious about auditioning this year.

Suddenly she felt a head next to her own. "Geez, she sounds like a teacher or something, lecturing you like that," a voice whispered in her ear.

Grace turned in surprise to see who was talking to her. It was the tall girl from bunk 3A. Up close, Grace could see that every inch of the girl's face, neck, and arms was covered in freckles. *Wow, she's even more freckly than me!* Grace thought.

"If you don't goof around, you'll get a part," the girl said in a fake high-pitched voice, making fun of Brynn.

Brynn shot her a nasty look and scooched farther away, but Grace couldn't help smiling. Brynn *did* sound like a nag sometimes. She always wanted Grace to be more serious about acting. Grace knew it was because Brynn thought she was talented. But still, sometimes her friend got a little too intense.

"You're in 3C, right?" the tall girl asked.

Grace nodded. "I'm Grace."

"I'm Gaby." She pulled her long brown hair back and tied it in a careless knot. "I'll forgive you for being in a lame bunk."

"Oh." Grace wasn't sure what to say. It was hard to tell if Gaby was kidding or not. "Thanks."

"Okay, everyone, let's get started!" Bethany, the drama instructor, strode into the room and stood in front of the group. She was tiny, with the wiry body of a dancer and wispy dark hair. But Grace knew from last summer that Bethany was a powerhouse when it came to acting. As soon as she got into a character, her whole appearance seemed to change. "I know what you're all wondering, so I'm just going to get it out of the way right now," Bethany went on. "The play this year will be *Peter Pan*."

Brynn turned to Grace excitedly. "I'm totally trying out for Wendy," she whispered.

"But that's a big part," Grace whispered back. "Are you sure?"

"Absolutely. How else am I going to get experience?" Brynn replied.

Gaby let out a loud snort. "You don't stand a chance," she said loudly. "Our CIT said that nobody from the third division ever gets a lead role. You're too young."

"Well then, *you're* too young to get a good part, too," Brynn shot back. "You're in the third division just like us."

"Girls!" Bethany interrupted. "I need everyone to pay attention. Now, for the record, any camper from any division is eligible for any role in the play. Since the beginning of the summer, all the kids who have taken drama have been given audition pieces to work on, so auditions aren't limited to just this class. You don't have to try out, but you can if you want to." She looked right at Brynn and Gaby. "No one is kept out because they're too young."

"Right. It's just because you're too dumb," cracked one of the boys from the fifth division.

"Speak for yourself," Brynn murmured.

Grace bit back a laugh. Brynn was usually really nice. But if you got on her bad side, she had no problem defending herself.

"I don't care what anyone says. I'm going to play Wendy," Brynn announced loudly.

Several of the other kids snickered or rolled their eyes. Grace sighed. She liked Brynn—she always had—but she had to admit that sometimes Brynn could get a little overbearing. During auditions last year, Brynn had spent one whole weekend being in character as Annie Oakley, just to get herself ready for her audition piece from *Annie Get Your Gun*. She wouldn't even speak to her bunkmates unless they called her "Annie." She called it "method acting." Apparently lots of famous celebrities use the technique to prepare for a role. Was 3C in for the same thing this year?

"Auditions are next Wednesday," Bethany went on. "There are two audition scenes to choose from for the girls and two for the boys. Everyone will have a partner, and your job is to help each other prepare. The first half hour of every class will be devoted to practicing for your auditions."

Grace leaned toward Brynn, but before she could say anything, she felt Gaby poke her in the side. She glanced over at the tall girl.

"Wanna be partners?" Gaby asked. "You're the only fun one here."

"Thanks, but . . ." Grace wasn't sure what to say. She'd assumed she would partner up with Brynn since they were bunkmates. But Brynn didn't even seem to have heard the whole "partner" speech. She was staring straight ahead, her lips moving as she recited a scene to herself. Grace knew all too well how being Brynn's partner would turn out—they'd spend all their free time working on their audition scenes, and Brynn would constantly tell Grace that she should practice more. It wouldn't be any fun at all. And besides, Brynn had Alex to help her practice.

Grace got the feeling that being partners with Brynn would really mean being partners with Brynn *and* her best friend. Except for free choice, Brynn and Alex were always together. Grace would just be the third wheel, the way she always seemed to end up with her bunkmates.

"Well?" Gaby was grinning at her, and Grace had to admit that it was flattering to know somebody wanted her as a partner. She barely knew Gaby at all because they never socialized with bunk 3A. But maybe that silly rivalry had cost her the chance to make a best friend at camp. Gaby was outgoing just like her, and Gaby seemed to want to have fun in drama, just like her. Why not partner up?

"Sure," she said. "It'll be a blast."

▲ ▲ ▲

"I can't believe you did that!" Brynn fumed. They were only ten feet away from their bunk, and Brynn had been yelling at Grace the whole way back from the drama shack.

"Shh!" Grace hissed. "Do you want everyone else to hear you?"

Brynn glanced up at bunk 3C. "Why should I care if they hear?" she asked. "I'm not the one who stabbed my friend in the back!"

Natalie's face appeared in the window, and Candace peered out the door. Grace sighed. Now her disagreement with Brynn would become a bunk-wide discussion. "I didn't mean to stab you in the back," she said for the fifth time. Brynn had been so busy ranting during the walk back that Grace didn't think she'd heard her the first four times. "I really, really didn't."

"What's going on?" Chelsea demanded, popping

out the door of the bunk. Whenever there was any kind of controversy, Chelsea was always the first one to stick her nose into it. "What are you guys fighting about?"

"Yeah, why are you fighting?" Candace asked, sounding much more concerned than Chelsea.

"We're not fighting," Grace said. "We're just . . . disagreeing."

"Oh, please," Chelsea said. "Brynn was totally yelling at you. You are too fighting."

"No we aren't," Brynn said immediately. "Grace and I are friends. We don't fight."

Grace had to smile. Sometimes when Chelsea was rude, it made everyone else band together to oppose her. "That's right," Grace said. "Brynn is just upset because I decided not to be her partner in drama."

"So that's how you stabbed her in the back?" Chelsea asked.

"She didn't mean to stab me in the back," Brynn retorted. "She was just being nice to this girl from 3A who asked her to be partners first. You know Grace— she can never say no to people. She thinks it will hurt their feelings."

Grace blinked in surprise. Apparently Brynn *had* heard her the first four times she'd tried to explain about Gaby and the drama class.

Brynn noticed her expression and laughed. "What?" she said. "I was upset so I wanted to vent. It doesn't mean I wasn't listening."

"Oh. Then do you need me to apologize again?" Grace asked. "Because I will. I never meant to insult you."

"I know," Brynn grumbled, heading inside. "You were just making a new friend. Still, I'm bummed that we won't be partners. What about our pact?"

"We can still audition together," Grace said.

"Okay." Brynn gave her a bright smile. But Grace felt nauseous. What if she couldn't audition? Wouldn't Brynn be even madder at her then?

I won't let that happen, Grace told herself. *Somehow I have to audition for the play.*

▲ ▲ ▲

"Hey, Grace!" Natalie called at free swim the next day. "Are you swimming?"

Grace wandered over to where Natalie had her whole setup on the little beach next to the lake. Nat was an excellent swimmer—she'd been placed in the highest level, blue, immediately, even though it was only her first summer here. But she almost never swam during free swim. She preferred to sun herself and read her fashion magazines. Grace plopped down on the edge of Natalie's super-huge towel.

"I don't know," she said. "My stomach's been hurting ever since breakfast this morning. I think I finally hit my limit on greasy sausages."

"Shh! Don't say that in front of Marissa," Natalie said. She nodded toward their CIT, who was on her way over to them.

Grace grinned. Marissa had served the less-than-tasty breakfast food, true. But it had been prepared by Pete, Camp Lakeview's official assistant cook. Last year he had been a counselor, but for some reason, this summer he'd decided to torture them by learning to cook. In spite of the bad food, everybody loved Pete. Especially Marissa. She did a bad job of hiding her crush on Pete—all the girls in 3C were sure they were secretly dating. Plus, Pete was a great guy. Grace didn't want to insult either of them.

"It's probably just a stomachache from stress, anyway," Grace said. "The stress of living through Brynn's wrath!"

Natalie giggled. "She was pretty mad at you yesterday. I can't believe you picked that 3A girl to be your drama partner over Brynn!"

"No, I didn't," Grace protested. "Gaby asked me first."

"Are we still talking about the drama in drama?" Marissa quipped as she reached them. She pulled out her own super-huge towel and spread it on the sand next to Natalie's. This had been their free-swim ritual since the second day of camp. It worked pretty well for everyone— you could always leave your stuff with Nat and Marissa while you went swimming.

"I didn't mean to be rude to Brynn," Grace said. "But she's so intense all the time, and I like acting because it's fun. We'd be bad partners. She's too serious and I'm not serious enough!"

"Well, I have to agree with that," Marissa said.

"Besides, why shouldn't I expand my horizons a little?" Grace added. "Who cares if I hang out with Gaby? Aren't we here at camp to make new friends?"

Natalie snorted. "You sound like my mother."

"I have *CosmoGIRL*, *Teen People*, and *Teen Vogue*," Marissa announced, pulling the magazines from her bag. "Who wants what?"

"Ugh, no *Teen People* for me," Natalie said, laughing. "I've had enough of celebrities."

"All right, it's *Teen Vogue* for you and *CosmoGIRL* for

Grace," Marissa said, handing over the thick mag. "It's the Back-to-School issue."

"No wonder it weighs five thousand pounds," Grace said, lugging the magazine toward her. "Back to school isn't back to school without three hundred pages of fashion advice."

"Don't forget the dating advice," Natalie said. "And the friendship advice, and the how-to-organize-your-locker advice . . ."

"And the makeup and the hair . . ." Marissa added.

Grace flopped back on the big towel and put the magazine over her face. "I really just wanted a sunshade," she joked. "That much advice will kill me!"

"I can't believe the start of school is so close," Natalie said. "It's only a month away!"

"Summer goes too fast," Marissa agreed.

Grace sat back up. School was the last thing she wanted to be talking about on a perfect summer day. "You guys, we still have half the summer left," she pointed out. "Who cares if the magazines come out early?"

"You're right." Natalie was flipping through hers. "Let's just find a fun quiz and forget about school."

"Now you're talking." Grace turned the pages until she found a quiz in her own magazine. "Here we go. 'How to Know If Your Love Will Last.' Well, Nat? Do you know if your love with Simon will last?"

Natalie swatted her while Marissa laughed. "No one said we are in love. You just wait until you find some cute boy, Grace."

"No thanks," Grace said. "Boys are nothing but trouble."

"You said it!" Gaby appeared next to them, her

tall form casting a long shadow over the blankets. "Mind if I sit?"

"Hang on." Grace grabbed her own towel and quickly spread it out. "Have a seat. I've been hogging Natalie's towel this whole time, and it's pretty comfortable."

"Good, then I'll hog yours!" Gaby folded her long legs and sat. "How come you're not swimming?" she asked Grace.

"My stomach feels a little funky. What about you?"

Gaby shrugged. "I just don't feel like it."

"Are you Grace's new drama partner?" Marissa asked.

"Yup! It's gonna be a nonstop party, right, Grace?"

"Absolutely," Grace said. "We should probably choose our audition scenes—we're supposed to tell Bethany tomorrow which ones we're doing."

"What are the choices?" Natalie asked.

"There's a scene from *The Music Man* and one from *The Sound of Music*," Grace said. "I think I'm going to do *The Sound of Music*. Maria has such a good sense of humor. I think I can play her really well."

"Whatever," Gaby said. "I'll do the same one you do. That way we can help each other remember the lines."

"Sounds good."

"Can we get back to the love quiz?" Natalie asked with mock annoyance. "I'm dying to know how I do."

"You're right. Free swim is for goofing around, not for drama talk!" Grace grabbed the magazine. She was just about to read the first question when Julie walked up with Tyler, the swimming counselor. As a rule, Grace didn't like boys. But Tyler was so good-looking that every girl at Lakeview liked him. He and Jenna's older sister,

Stephanie, were sort of an item.

"This looks like a party," Julie said with a smile. "What are you guys doing?"

"Magazine quizzes," Marissa told her. "You know how Nat loves the quizzes."

"Yeah, but what about you, Grace?" Tyler asked. "You're usually the first one in the lake."

"I know, but I thought I'd take it easy today," Grace replied. "I'm trying out the lie-in-the-sun-and-read-magazines approach. Natalie and Marissa always look so relaxed and happy after free swim."

"Weren't you reading a book the other day?" Julie asked. "What ever happened to that?"

Grace felt her face heat up, and it wasn't from the sun. "I didn't bring it with me," she said. "I was expecting to swim."

"Tyler!" A voice from the lake interrupted them. It was Stephanie. "Come judge our swimming race! I'm too biased."

Jenna and her twin brother, Adam, waved from the water. Obviously they were the ones preparing to race—both of them were all-around great athletes. But their own sister couldn't call a race for them.

"Be right there!" Tyler yelled back. He turned to Julie. "Wanna help judge?"

"Why not?" she said cheerfully. "See you guys later!" They took off toward the lake.

"Wow, your counselor is big on reading, huh?" Gaby asked when Julie was gone.

"I guess so," Grace told her. She really didn't want to talk about boring books with her new friend—or about why Julie wanted her to read. "What's your counselor like?"

"Lizzie? She's cool." Gaby glanced around the beach. "Although if she catches me talking to all you 3C girls, she'll tease me all night! I'd better go. I just wanted to say hi."

"Okay," Grace told her. "I'll see you in drama tomorrow."

"You got it, partner!" Gaby waved and headed off to find some of her bunkmates.

"Well, well, well," Natalie said, nudging Grace with her shoulder. "Consorting with the enemy, are we?"

Grace smiled. "Yes, we are. That rivalry is just for fun."

"I agree. Gaby seems nice," Natalie said. "But I'm still waiting for the quiz."

"Me too," Marissa chimed in.

"All right, here we go." Grace read the first question for her friends. She was determined not to think about what Julie had said. After all, the sun was shining, she was having fun with her bunkmates, and best of all, she had a brand-new friend!

chapter
THREE

"Bunk 5D has Bunk Day on Thursday . . ."

"Psst, Grace!" Valerie whispered from across the table. "Want my hash browns?"

Grace shook her head. All of her bunkmates were holding whispered conversations around her. Nobody ever paid attention to the daily breakfast announcements that Dr. Steve, the head of Camp Lakeview, made. At least not until they heard their own bunk mentioned.

"How about you, Alex?" Valerie asked. "Want my hash browns?"

"No thanks," Alex said quickly. "I'm not hungry."

"You're *never* hungry," Jenna grumbled.

"And the cookout tonight will be for bunk 2B . . . or not to be!"

Dr. Steve got more groans than laughter for his lame joke. Grace glanced over at Brynn, who was now reciting the rest of the "to be or not to be" speech to herself. "I knew it," Grace joked to Alyssa, who sat next to her. "Brynn has gone into total drama mode. Every little thing that happens from now until her audition for the play will be about acting."

"Don't remind me," Jenna said from the other side of Grace. "Remember last year when she tried to lock us all out of the bunk so she could rehearse in private?"

Grace giggled. "She actually dragged one of the counselors' cots over in front of the door to block it."

"But the door opens outward, so it totally didn't work," Jenna finished for her. "We just opened the door and climbed over the bed!"

Natalie laughed, while Alyssa studied Brynn for a moment. "She's really focused," Alyssa finally said. "But from what I hear, you're just as talented as she is, Grace."

". . . a special treat for the third division." Dr. Steve's voice broke into their conversation. Grace spun around to watch him. His balding head looked a little sunburned—he must have forgotten to wear his usual fishing hat yesterday.

"As you all know, the second division and the fourth division have already had their field trips this year," Dr. Steve said.

Jenna grabbed Grace's arm excitedly. "Field trip!" she whispered.

"Now it's the third division's turn," Dr. Steve went on. "Next Thursday you kids will be going to WetWorld, the new water park up in Norwich."

Cheering erupted all around Grace, so she joined right in. In fact, she even climbed onto the bench to celebrate. Two tables over, she saw Gaby do the same thing. They waved to each other over all the clapping and jumping campers.

"Water park! That is so cool," Jenna cried. "I hear they have a three-story-high waterslide!"

"You'll do *that*, but you were afraid to dive off the three-foot-high board?" Chelsea sniffed.

Jenna ignored her, but Grace couldn't keep quiet. Sometimes Chelsea could be really nasty. "Jenna's not afraid of diving anymore," she said. "And I bet you won't go on the giant waterslide."

"Yeah," Candace agreed. "I bet you won't."

Chelsea frowned. "It would ruin my hair. Think of all the chlorine in places like that."

"You're going to have to avoid the whole park if you don't want to get chlorine in your hair," Valerie pointed out.

"Whatever. I'm sure there's a wave pool I can lounge by."

"Not me," Grace said. "I'm going on every single ride in the park. Twice, if I have time!"

Her bunkmates laughed.

"That's okay. Karen will hang out with me and not go in the water. Right, Karen?" Chelsea asked, turning to the shy girl.

Karen didn't look too happy with that prospect, but she nodded. "Sure," she said quietly. Chelsea smiled, satisfied.

Grace frowned. Why did Karen always go along with anything Chelsea said? She obviously didn't want to spend her time at the water park sitting on a lounge chair. But it was always that way with the two of them—Chelsea called the shots. "You guys are crazy," Grace told them. "One day in the pool water isn't going to do anything to your hair. And besides, it would be worth looking like the Bride of Frankenstein to go on the rides!" She pulled the elastic off her ponytail and quickly teased her hair with her fingers. It never took much to make her mass of red curls stand on end. Within five seconds, she had a mop of hair standing straight up.

Everyone cracked up. Even Chelsea. And, more importantly, even Karen.

Out of the corner of her eye, Grace noticed Kathleen, the head counselor for the third division, leaning over to talk to Julie. Julie always ate with the bunk, sitting at the head of their table. But Kathleen sat with the other division heads, up at the table in the front of the room. What was she doing here? Neither she nor Julie were smiling. It didn't seem as if they were talking about the water park.

"Hey, Grace, have you ever gone on one of those inner-tube rides?" Jenna asked.

"Um, yeah," Grace said, dragging her attention away from Kathleen and Julie. "That's always my favorite ride at water parks. I love when you get to the end and you go down that little tunnel thing. It feels like you're being flushed down the drain!"

Everyone was still laughing, but Grace felt a sinking feeling of dread as she noticed Julie winding through the happy campers toward her.

"Grace, can I talk to you for a sec?" she called over the din.

Grace didn't answer. She just followed Julie toward the door of the mess hall. The sounds of hooting and cheering were all around her, but right now the water park seemed very far away.

"Where have you been?" Alex asked when Grace

got back to the bunk. It was chore time, and everyone was busy sweeping, dusting, or cleaning the bathroom.

"Yeah, what did Julie want?" Chelsea added. "Are you in trouble or something?"

"No, but thanks for asking," Grace mumbled. As if she didn't feel bad enough already!

Alex rolled her eyes and gave Grace a smile. "Never mind," she said. "You better get going—it's your turn to take out the garbage."

"Whoo-hoo," Grace joked halfheartedly. But it wasn't the garbage that was bothering her. It was the memory of her meeting with Julie and Kathleen. She'd been expecting the worst, and that's what she'd gotten. All she wanted to do was hide under her sheets. If her bunkmates found out what was going on, she would be humiliated.

And Chelsea was still watching her like a hawk.

Grace quickly headed over to the cubby where the trash bags were kept and pulled out one for the bathroom garbage and one for the main-bunk garbage. Usually she liked to sing or whistle while doing chores—it got the other girls giggling, and sometimes they joined in. But today she just wasn't in the mood.

"Hang on a second!" Sarah cried as Grace picked up the bathroom garbage can. "I have a handful of hair to throw in there." Sarah wore the bunk's giant, blue rubber gloves, but she still picked hair out of the shower drain with two fingers, holding it away from herself as if it might attack her. "In fact, I think it's your hair," she added, scrunching up her face in disgust.

Grace squinted at the mass of red hair dangling from Sarah's outstretched hand. It could just as easily have been Alyssa's hair, but she decided not to mention that. She just wanted to get her chores over with as soon as possible so that she could go outside and forget about her bad morning.

"After chores, Brynn's going to do a dramatic reading of her *Music Man* scene for the play audition," Sarah told her, dumping the hair in Grace's garbage bag.

Brynn stuck her head out of the toilet area, where she was scrubbing the bowls. "Yeah," she added. "Why don't you join me? We can do it together. Or are you going to do *The Sound of Music* for your audition?"

Grace's stomach felt heavy, as if she had swallowed a handful of rocks. "Um, I don't think I'm gonna audition for the play after all," she said. "I'll just do stage crew again, or whatever Bethany makes us do as part of the drama class."

"What?" Brynn came all the way out into the bathroom. Grace quickly turned and headed into the main bunk, but it was no good. Brynn followed her. "What are you talking about?" Brynn demanded. "You have to audition! You're really good. What about our pact?"

Grace lifted the trash bag and made an exaggerated sour expression. "Sorry, I'm really grossed out by this garbage," she said, trying to sound like she was holding her breath to avoid smelling the junk. "I have to go dump it." She hurried across the bunk and pushed through the door, into the sunshine.

As soon as she was away from bunk 3C, Grace slowed down. She was in no rush to get back. Her bunkmates thought of her as the clown, always bubbly and up for fun. But right now, she couldn't imagine joking around . . . and she certainly couldn't imagine having fun!

She threw the garbage bags into the huge Dumpster near the camp office, then turned to go back. To her surprise, Gaby was trudging up the path toward the Dumpster.

"Hey," Grace said. "You're on garbage duty, too, huh?"

"Yeah, I tried to get out of it, but no one would trade with me," Gaby answered. She held out one of her two full trash bags. Grace grabbed it and hoisted it into the Dumpster while Gaby threw the other one in. They started back down the trail that led to the bunks.

"So what's your problem?" Gaby asked.

Grace was so startled that she almost tripped over a maple root in the path. "Huh?"

"Your problem," Gaby repeated. "You've been moping around all morning. I saw you acting all miserable on your way back from the office earlier, and even now you look like you just ate something sour."

"Well, I did have bug juice at breakfast," Grace joked.

"Funny. Not," Gaby said, completely deadpan.

For the first time in her life, Grace was speechless. She couldn't tell if Gaby was being rude or friendly. Her tone wasn't very nice, that much was certain. But in a way, she was asking if Grace was all right. And that *was* nice. Wasn't it?

"I guess I'm just in a bad mood," Grace finally said.

They had reached the clearing in the woods where all the bunks were. Grace slowed down, automatically taking a step or two away from Gaby. She came from their rival bunk, after all. A few of Grace's friends had already commented on the fact that she was consorting with the enemy. She didn't feel like having to defend herself to 3C right now. She knew they were only teasing, but the situation with her parents had her mega-stressed-out. So stressed that even joking around with her bunkmates seemed hard. "Um, I'll see you in drama," she muttered, speeding up.

"Wait!" Gaby called.

Grace turned back.

"Do you want to hang out during siesta this afternoon?" Gaby asked. "We can practice scenes or something."

Hang out during siesta? Grace could hardly believe her ears. Girls from 3A and 3C did not hang out together. It was an unspoken rule. And Gaby wanted to break it. *How can I say no without offending her?* Grace wondered. Should *I say no?*

"Come on, we'll have fun," Gaby prodded.

Grace glanced over at her bunk. Most of her bunkmates were lounging around on the steps or at the one dilapidated picnic table out front. Natalie was doing Alyssa's nails. Alex was reading lines with Brynn. Candace and Jessie were laughing over a magazine. Valerie and Sarah were practicing some kind of backflip. And Karen was French-braiding Chelsea's hair. They were all paired up, happy in their best-friend twosomes. There was nowhere for Grace to fit in.

How come she had never noticed this before?

"Earth to Grace. Please return to Camp Lakeview," Gaby said in a fake deep voice. "Are we hanging later or not?"

"Why not?" Grace said. It wasn't like her bunkmates would care. They already had their camp best friends.

Obviously it was time for Grace to get one, too. And Gaby was the only one who seemed interested, even if she was a little hard to figure out sometimes. "I'll meet you here."

"Cool." Gaby started walking backward toward bunk 3A. "Later."

"Later," Grace answered happily.

Grace's happiness didn't last long. As soon as the bunk sat down for lunch in the mess hall, Chelsea turned to her. "You never told us what Julie wanted this morning," she said loudly. "Or was it Kathleen who wanted to talk to you?"

Grace froze with a forkful of bright orange mac and cheese halfway to her mouth. She really didn't want to talk about that, especially not with the whole bunk listening. In fact, all she wanted to do was forget about this morning.

Natalie and Alyssa exchanged a look. "Who cares what they wanted?" Natalie said. "Let's talk about the field trip to WetWorld. I say we go on all the rides together. You know, to show our bunk 3C spirit!"

"Yeah, let's show our spirit," Candace agreed. Grace couldn't help smiling. You could always count on Candace for support. She never had much to say on her own, so she usually just repeated what everyone else said—as long as it was something nice.

"But then what's Grace going to do?" Chelsea asked. "Her new best friend is from 3A. She'll have to be in two places at once!"

A few of the girls laughed, and even Brynn and Alex smiled.

Grace felt her face get hot. She knew her friends weren't really mad at her for hanging out with Gaby. But Chelsea wasn't just teasing—she was being snotty. She was always rude, and everyone in 3C knew it. So why were they laughing along with her as if she was just making a joke?

Grace dropped her fork back down to her plate. She'd had enough of Chelsea's nosiness and her attitude. If her other friends weren't going to defend her, she'd just have to defend herself. "Maybe if my bunkmates acted more like friends are supposed to, I wouldn't have to look for a best friend in 3A," she snapped.

Then she got up and stormed out of the mess hall, ignoring Nat and Brynn calling after her. How dare Chelsea try to tell her who to be friends with!

Once she got outside, though, her stomach did a little flip. Had she really just yelled at all her bunkmates? They hadn't meant to upset her, and she knew it. She'd probably even been too harsh to Chelsea.

Grace sighed. She wasn't mad at them. She was mad at herself, and she'd taken it out on them. How had she gotten herself into this mess?

"But I don't understand," Grace said the next day in drama class. She was using a thick British accent and a deep voice. "How could a mouse have unlocked the door?"

"Maybe he had a key," Brynn answered shrilly. She stood on top of one of the black boxes, pretending it was a chair.

"A mouse with a key? Preposterous!" Grace bellowed. "Everybody knows mice never use keys. They prefer to ring the doorbell!" She saw a tiny smile flicker across Brynn's face, but Brynn quickly squelched it. Even though the improvisation exercise they were doing was silly, they both had to take it seriously in order to stay in character. It was hard, though, considering that all their classmates were laughing out loud.

"All I know is that a horrible little mouse came in and stole all the cheese from my kitchen," Brynn cried in her best imitation of a frightened old lady.

Grace's character was supposed to be a gruff police detective. Making him British was a little addition of her own. She loved the improv part of drama because they were allowed to add personal touches like that to spice things up. Picturing a burly English inspector in her mind, she pretended to pull a notebook from her pocket. "Can you describe the mouse?" she asked in her fake voice.

"It was small and gray with a twitchy nose," Brynn said. She added a shudder for effect.

"I see." Grace pretended to write that down. "And can you describe the cheese?"

One of the boys laughed loudly. Grace caught sight of him out of the corner of her eye. He was very tan, with short blond hair and a friendly smile. His green eyes gleamed with amusement as he watched her.

"Ahem!" Brynn said loudly. Grace jumped. Brynn was staring at her, obviously expecting an answer. But Grace hadn't even heard a word Brynn said.

"Oh!" Grace cried. "I'm sorry. I was distracted by . . ." *Think fast,* she told herself. *I can't say I was distracted by a boy.* ". . . by that mouse. I think it's your culprit!" She pointed to a spot on the floor near Brynn's black box.

Brynn gave a little scream and stood up on her tiptoes to get even farther away from the "mouse."

Grace swooped down and pretended to pick it up by its tail. She squinted into thin air and nodded wisely. "This mouse is the thief."

"How can you tell?" Brynn asked.

How can I tell? Grace wondered. She thought fast. "It has cheese breath," she announced.

Everybody laughed again, and most of the other campers applauded. Bethany joined in the applause as she walked toward Grace and Brynn at the front of the room. "Well done," she said. "That was an excellent improvisation."

Grace glanced over at Brynn, who was beaming. She could feel the huge smile on her own face, too. Bethany had assigned each of them a character—the old lady and the detective—and given them the word "mouse." Everything else they made up on the spot.

"If you try out and get a role in the play, this is the kind of applause you'll get," Brynn murmured. "And it will be even more fun than the scene we just did." She'd been trying to convince Grace to audition ever since Grace had said she wasn't going to try out. Grace couldn't tell Brynn the real reason she had to skip auditions, so she'd found herself avoiding her friend outside of drama class. It was awful.

Grace pretended she hadn't heard Brynn's comment. "We're a good team," she said as they took their seats with their classmates.

"Yeah, too bad you decided not to be my partner," Brynn teased her. Grace knew her bunkmate had been annoyed at first, but Brynn seemed to like her new partner just fine. His name was Peter, and Grace had to admit that he was pretty cute.

Her gaze wandered over to the blond boy who'd been laughing so loudly during their scene. To her surprise, he was looking right back at her. He gave her a smile and a thumbs-up. Shocked, Grace sat back so that she was hidden by Brynn. She leaned over to Gaby, who sat on the other side of her.

"Who's that boy with the blond hair?" she asked.

Gaby immediately craned her neck to look over at him. "Devon Something," she said. "He's in 3F. Why?"

"He really liked our improv. He was laughing the

whole time."

"Well, it was pretty ridiculous," Gaby said.

Grace didn't answer. She still had a hard time figuring out whether or not Gaby was kidding sometimes.

"That's it for today," Bethany said. "Next time we'll be doing movie scenes." As everybody got up and began heading for the door, Bethany pulled Grace aside.

"Your scene was really funny," she said. "Have you done improv exercises before?"

"Only once. In Drama Club at school," Grace said.

"Well, you're a natural." Bethany smiled. "I hope you're planning to audition for the play."

Grace hesitated. "I don't know. I'm only in the third division."

"I meant what I said, Grace. Anyone from any division can audition." Bethany raised an eyebrow. "Just because a third-level camper has never gotten a lead before doesn't mean it can't happen."

Grace wasn't sure how to answer. Had Julie and Kathleen talked to Bethany? It didn't seem like it. For a brief moment Grace considered trying to lie to the drama teacher. Maybe if Bethany didn't know . . .

But Grace was no liar. She knew she couldn't do that.

"Just think about it," Bethany added. "Someone as talented as you are should really try out."

"Okay," Grace said. She forced a smile onto her face and left. If only people would stop telling her how talented she was! It only made her feel worse that she couldn't audition for the play.

By the time Grace got into her bathing suit and made it to the lake, free swim had already started. Talking to Bethany had made her late, and she'd had to stop at the camp office on the way back to the bunk.

To her surprise, she spotted Natalie in the water with Alyssa. Natalie almost never went in during free swim, but it was unusually hot today. Obviously her latest fashion magazine could wait until after she'd cooled down. Jenna was swimming laps with her brother Adam, and Brynn and Alex were hanging out in a pair of inner tubes, talking. Well, Brynn was talking. Alex just bobbed in the water, listening intently and nodding. She wasn't saying a word. *Brynn must be practicing her audition scene with Alex as the audience,* Grace thought. *I wish Emily was here. She'd let me practice with her like that, too.*

A flicker of guilt stabbed at her. She still hadn't finished that letter to her best friend. Grace kicked the sand in frustration. She didn't seem able to do anything right this summer!

She tossed her towel onto the ground and stuck her toe in the water. Camp Lakeview rules stated that no one could go in the lake without a swimming buddy, even for free swim. The counselors were pretty flexible about that rule, though. As long as campers didn't swim alone, the counselors didn't care how many buddies they had. Which was good when you were best-friendless. Grace squinted across the sparkling water toward her friends. Maybe she'd ask Nat and Alyssa if she could triple with them.

"Hey, Gracie," Gaby said from behind her. "You're late. I was waiting for you to be my swim buddy."

"Oh." *Gracie?* Grace thought. *Why is she calling me that?* She noticed that Gaby had already dumped her own towel right next to Grace's.

"Let's go," Gaby prodded. "I'm dying from this heat." She waded into the shallow end of the lake without a backward glance. Grace almost yelled after her—Gaby would be in trouble if she swam without a partner. But obviously Gaby was assuming Grace would follow her.

It was kind of weird. Gaby hadn't even asked Grace if she *wanted* to be swim buddies. She'd just decided that they would be, and she expected Grace to go along with that. It was sort of rude. But again, it was also sort of flattering. Maybe Gaby simply figured that they were good enough friends that she didn't have to ask. That's how Grace acted with Emily at home. It was the sort of thing that best friends did.

"Wait up," Grace called, splashing in after Gaby.

▲ ▲ ▲

"Are you kidding?"

It was just before lights-out that night, and Chelsea was looming next to Grace's bed looking extremely demanding. As usual.

Grace marked her page with her finger and looked at Chelsea. Karen hovered behind her, carrying Chelsea's makeup bag. Grace had never figured out why Chelsea had to take the bag to the bathroom every night to wash off her makeup, but maybe there was some kind of magic face-cleaner stuff in there.

"What are you talking about?" Grace asked.

"That book." Chelsea snatched it out of Grace's hands, losing Grace's place. Grace groaned. Now she'd never find the right page again. "Why are you pretending to read *The Call of the Wild?*" Chelsea asked.

"I'm not pretending," Grace said indignantly. "Why

would I fake reading?"

"Because there's no way you'd want to read a book at night. You're always the first one to answer every single magazine quiz question that Marissa asks," Chelsea replied.

A few of the other girls giggled. Grace couldn't argue. The truth was, she would much rather listen to Marissa's nightly reading from some magazine article or quiz. The book she was reading was boring with a capital B. But she had no choice. Marissa was settled on her own cot and ready to start reading aloud, but Grace was going to have to ignore her and read *The Call of the Wild*.

But that didn't mean she wanted to talk about it. Especially not with Chelsea. She held out her hand. "May I have my book back?"

Chelsea shrugged and handed it to her. Grace rolled over on her stomach and flipped through the book, trying to find her place again. She skimmed the paragraphs, but they all blurred together in her mind. It was impossible to remember which parts she had read and which she hadn't. *I guess I haven't been paying much attention to what I've been reading,* she thought. Finally she just gave up, picked a likely place, and began reading again.

"The movie will begin filming in October and is expected to be released next summer," Marissa's voice drifted into Grace's attention.

"That is so amazing!" Sarah cried. "I can't believe your dad is making another 'spy' movie, Nat."

"Yeah, I thought he said he wanted to do more serious roles from now on," Brynn put in.

"He always says that. It's just a way of negotiating with the producers," Natalie explained.

Grace found herself staring down at the page, reading the word "Yukon" over and over while she half listened to her bunkmates' conversation.

"I can't believe we have to wait until next summer to see it, though," Valerie was saying. "That's *forever*."

"Can't you tell us what the plot is?" Brynn asked.

"Yeah, tell us what the plot is," Candace put in.

"I'm not allowed to," Natalie said. "Dad has a confidentiality clause in his contract. He can't even tell *me* everything about the plot."

Everybody groaned.

"Tell you what, though," Natalie went on. "I can ask Dad for a few sneak previews. He's allowed to take pictures on location—he's an amateur photographer, so he takes his camera with him everywhere."

"Wow, he's really multitalented," Alex breathed.

"He's *so* multitalented," Candace agreed.

"As long as the photos don't show the sets or let you figure out what the plot is, I can mail them out to you guys," Natalie said. "It'll be pictures of him having dinner with the director, hanging out with the other actors . . . stuff like that."

"And you'll send them to us?" Valerie cried.

"I promise," Nat said.

That did it. Grace let the book close and sat up in her bed to join in the cheering. What was the point of reading some old, boring book when there was juicy Hollywood gossip to discuss?

"Cool! And we can send pictures from camp to his movie set," she said. "What do you think?" Grace jumped out of bed and struck a pose in the middle of the room, putting her hand on her hip and pursing her lips like a supermodel.

"I think you look like a fish," Chelsea muttered.

But the other girls laughed, and Sarah leapt up to stand next to Grace in the same silly position. "Someone take a picture," she joked.

"Everyone join in!" Grace called. "Then Nat can send the photo to her dad, and the director will see it, and we'll all be discovered."

"The fish-face girls of bunk 3C," Alyssa said, cracking up.

As her friends jumped around, striking other dumb model poses, Grace felt a rush of happiness. This kind of silly stuff was what camp was all about.

She'd read her book tomorrow.

"Check it out. There's Natalie and her *boyfriend*," Sarah announced as they all filed into the mess hall for lunch the next day. She spoke loudly, clearly wanting Natalie to hear. Simon's bunk, 3F, ate at a table only a few feet away from bunk 3C's table.

But Natalie just kept talking to Simon as if she hadn't noticed. Grace wondered how she could stay so calm when people were teasing her—especially with Simon sitting right there.

"Yeah, and I think Alyssa's boyfriend is over there, too," Jenna added loudly.

Grace laughed. "You're talking about your own brother," she pointed out. "I don't think you get to make fun of Alyssa for liking *him*."

"Are you kidding? He's the last boy anyone should like." Jenna pretended to bump into her twin brother, Adam, as she walked by bunk 3F's table. But Adam was too fast for her. He grabbed her and gave her a noogie.

"That's one way to handle it," said a voice from behind her.

Grace jumped and turned to see Devon, the

blond boy from drama class. "Oh. Um . . ." Grace's heart pounded. She couldn't think of a single word.

"The guys in our bunk are always teasing Simon, and now they tease Adam, too," Devon said. "At least when it's his sister doing the teasing, he can stop her!"

"Yeah." Grace couldn't remember whether she and Devon had ever spoken to each other. "I'm Grace," she said.

Devon looked a little confused, and instantly she felt like an idiot. He hadn't asked her name. He'd been talking about Simon and Adam!

"I know," he said. "We're in drama together."

"Oh." Grace stared into his big eyes and tried to come up with anything to say. But all she could think about was the fact that the back of her neck felt sweaty and hot, and her heart kept slamming against her rib cage. What was going on with her?

"I'm Devon," he said. He stuck out his hand to shake. "I guess we haven't really met officially."

Grace stared at his hand in horror. She hadn't realized it until now, but her palms were totally sweaty, too. How could she shake his hand when hers were all wet?

"Enough with the romance!" Alex cried, pushing in between Grace and Devon so she could get to Natalie. "Tear yourself away from the boys, and come sit down and eat."

Grace wasn't exactly sure how it happened, but all of a sudden Natalie, Alyssa, Jenna, and Alex were all coming back from 3F's table, talking and laughing. They pulled Grace along with them, yanking her away before she had a chance to shake Devon's hand.

She glanced over her shoulder to see Devon

watching. Did he think she'd just snubbed him on purpose? Had she accidentally been really rude?

Devon stuck his hand in his pocket and shrugged. But he was smiling.

▲ ▲ ▲

"I read this book about acting that said an actor's true job is to audition," Brynn said as they ate.

"What is *that* supposed to mean?" Grace asked. She stirred the meat loaf surprise around on her plate. The surprise seemed to be that it barely resembled any meat loaf she'd ever eaten.

"Just that actors spend a lot more time auditioning for roles than actually playing those roles," Brynn explained.

"It's true," Natalie put in. "My dad used to go to hundreds of auditions every year and sometimes he'd only get one part, if that."

"Wow. I bet he's happy he doesn't have to go through that anymore," Grace said.

Natalie shrugged. "He figures someday he won't be such a big star anymore, and then they'll expect him to try out again. For now, he's just enjoying the fact that he gets offered roles without auditioning."

"I can't believe *you're* not an actor, Nat," Karen said quietly. "You know everything about Hollywood."

"Seriously, you know everything," Candace agreed.

"Ugh, no," Natalie cried. "I would never want to live that way. Most actors spend their whole lives being waiters and never making enough money to live on. My father just got lucky."

"I don't care if I have to be a waitress," Brynn said. "As long as I can practice my craft."

Grace shoved a bite of the meat loaf into her mouth to hide her smile. Across the table, she saw Alyssa quickly look down to keep her own smile from showing. Everyone knew how serious Brynn was about becoming an actor. But it was still hard to imagine her carrying trays of food and waiting on other people. Maybe in four or five years she'd be a CIT like Marissa, and she'd get to practice being a waitress all summer long.

"Who wants my pudding?" Alex asked. It was a daily ritual—Alex never ate her dessert.

"Me!" Sarah cried, reaching for the little cup of chocolate pudding. She spooned a bite into her mouth and made a "yum!" face. "Are you ready for your audition, Brynn?" she asked. "You've been rehearsing nonstop."

"I have my lines memorized, but I still have to practice my song more," Brynn said. "How about you, Grace?"

The meat loaf seemed to get stuck halfway down Grace's throat. She'd been hoping no one would ask her about the play, but she should've known that Brynn wasn't going to just drop it. Even though Grace had broken their pact to audition together, Brynn still kept trying to keep up her end. She really wanted Grace to try out. "Um, I'm still not sure I'm going to audition," she mumbled.

Her bunkmates all gasped. "Why not?" Natalie asked. "You're such a good actress."

"Well, that's just the problem," Grace replied fake seriously. She waved them all in closer as if she had a big secret to tell. Once she had everyone's attention, she lowered her voice and said, "I don't want to embarrass all the other campers who can't act at all."

Everyone laughed. "How thoughtful of you," Natalie teased.

"You really aren't going to try out?" Jenna asked. "I mean, I know how competitive it is, but you could probably get a role as a Lost Boy or something."

"Or a pirate," Valerie said.

"Last year Brynn was the only one from our division to get a part at all, remember?" Alex pointed out. "The good roles always go to the older kids."

"But we're a year older now," Brynn said. "And I don't care how it's always been before. This year someone from the third division is definitely getting a part—me! I'm playing Wendy, and that's all there is to it. And Grace can play Tinkerbell!"

Grace couldn't help admiring Brynn's self-confidence. She was so determined to get a part that she might make it happen through sheer force of will. "You know, Brynn, Peter Pan is usually played by a woman," she said. "The character is a boy, but lots of times they get women to play the role."

"Yeah, all the famous Broadway Peter Pans were women," Natalie agreed.

"Maybe you should try out for Peter instead of Wendy," Grace suggested.

Brynn wrinkled her nose. "I don't know if I want to play a boy. Boys are kinda gross."

"But it would be a good acting challenge," Grace said. Everyone giggled.

"Maybe." Brynn didn't sound convinced.

"I could help you practice," Jenna offered. "I know all about being a boy from living with my brother. I can teach you how to belch in public and everything."

Grace watched as her bunkmates laughed and joked around with Brynn. She wanted to get into the spirit of it, but she couldn't stop thinking about the play auditions. She desperately wanted to try out for a role. And she hated the feeling that she was letting Brynn down. But unless her situation changed very, very quickly, she knew she wouldn't be able to audition no matter how much she wanted to.

"Mail call!" Julie yelled, pushing open the screen door with her hip. Her arms were filled with boxes and envelopes.

"Cool! What'd I get?" Jenna demanded, rushing over to grab the biggest box. It had the Bloom family's trademark giant orange stickers on it, which meant it was a care package from Jenna's mom. She always sent enough food for the whole bunk.

"I can't wait to find out—I'm starving," Julie joked. She plopped the rest of the mail down on her cot and began handing it out.

"Nat, a postcard from Tunisia," she called.

"My father's on location there," Natalie explained, taking the oversized card.

"Care package for Karen," Julie went on. "And letters for Valerie, Candace, Alison, and Grace."

Everyone else bounded happily over to get their mail, but Grace was in no rush. She had a feeling the letter was from her mother, and a letter from her mother wasn't a good thing, not this summer. *Maybe it's from Emily*, she thought hopefully. *I would have a great time reading about all the gossip from home.* But she knew her best friend wasn't going to write again so soon. Grace still hadn't answered Emily's first three letters.

She shuffled over to the counselor, hoping against hope that Emily had found out something so juicy that she simply had to write to Grace.

Julie gave her a sympathetic smile as she handed over the envelope.

Uh-oh, that face could only mean one thing, Grace thought. *It's a letter from Mom.*

Grace threw herself down on her bunk and slowly peeled open the envelope. The letter was short, and it said exactly what she had expected it to say. Usually Grace liked to read letters two or three times before she put them away, but not this letter. She stuck it right back into its envelope and slipped it into the box under her bed where she kept her unused stationery and the other letters from her folks and Emily. Then she rolled over on her bed and faced the wall. Even though she'd only read it once, the letter stuck in her mind. Especially the part that said "we're so disappointed in you." Tears pricked at her eyes. She hoped her bunkmates would leave her alone.

No such luck. "Grace? You okay?" Sarah asked from her own bunk.

"I'm fine," Grace replied. She turned back over and plastered a fake smile on her face.

"Are you sure?" Chelsea asked, leaning forward to peer closely at Grace. "Because you look kinda green."

"Thanks," Grace said. "I was going for yellow, but I guess I went a little too far."

A few of the other girls giggled, but Grace could see that Sarah, Alyssa, and Nat weren't convinced that she was kidding. Usually she could joke her way out of any situation, but right now she actually *felt* kinda green, if that was possible. She wasn't really sick, but she was worried and upset. Julie was still over at her own cot, but if she heard the girls talking about Grace's problem, she'd come over to investigate. And then everyone would find out her secret, and they would think she was a loser. *I have to get out of here before Julie gets involved,* Grace decided.

Natalie was opening her mouth to say something—probably something like, "What's really bothering you, Grace?"—but Grace was too fast for her. She leapt up off her bunk and stuck her feet in her flip-flops, all in one motion. "I'm gonna take a walk," she said, cutting Natalie off. "I don't feel like siesta-ing today."

She raced for the door and made it outside before anyone could answer. But what was she supposed to do now? She'd come outside without her book, and almost all of the other campers were in their bunks taking a siesta.

I wish I'd brought my letter to Emily so I could finish it, Grace thought. If only her best friend were here, she'd know how to cheer Grace up. But Emily was far away at home, and Grace was on her own.

Without really planning to, she started down the path toward bunk 3A. Maybe Gaby would want to hang out. That's what best friends did, right? And they were starting to be best friends. Camp best friends, anyway.

Bunk 3A looked exactly like bunk 3C, except that the sign on the door had different names written on it, and the porch had only one step leading up to it instead of two. Grace jumped over the step and landed on the porch. She stared at the door for a second. Was she supposed to knock? All of last summer, and all of this summer so far, she'd never gone to another bunk—unless she was on a raid with her bunkmates. You definitely didn't knock when you were raiding. But how about when you were just visiting? She had no idea what the etiquette was. She'd never needed friends outside her own bunk before.

She took a deep breath and lifted her hand to knock. Before she even touched the door, a short girl with long dark hair pushed it open. She stared at Grace in surprise.

"Uh, hi, Sharon," Grace said.

Sharon raised her eyebrows. "Hi, Grace," she said loudly. Obviously she wanted her bunkmates to hear her. Grace took a step back as a couple of the other 3A girls appeared behind Sharon. They stared at her curiously.

"Is she alone?" one of them whispered. "I bet it's a trick."

Great. They think I'm here to pull a prank or something, Grace thought. "Is Gaby here?" she asked.

Sharon's eyebrows shot up higher. "Gaby?" she asked, sounding even more surprised than she looked. "Yeah. Do you . . . do you want to see her?"

"Yup. Thanks," Grace said. These girls were acting even weirder than usual. Was it really that big a deal for a 3C girl to come to the door? Maybe she should've thought this through a little more.

She heard Gaby's voice from inside, along with a lot of giggling and whispering. Finally Gaby stepped up to the door. She shot Sharon a look. "Thanks. You can go back in," she said.

Sharon nodded, but she didn't move. Clearly she wanted to know why Grace was there.

Gaby rolled her eyes, turning to Grace. She looked

her up and down and frowned. "What are *you* doing here?" she demanded.

Grace hesitated. "Um . . . me?" she asked. Immediately she felt stupid. Who else would Gaby be talking to? But the question had taken her by surprise. She'd been expecting a "hello" or a "what's up"—not such a rude welcome from Gaby.

Gaby pushed the door open wider and stepped out onto the porch. A few of the other girls crowded around behind her. "Duh, of course I mean you," Gaby said. "Do you see anyone else who isn't supposed to be here?"

Grace's mouth dropped open. "Am I not supposed to be here?" she asked, confused. Had she missed some kind of no-visiting-during-siesta rule?

"No one from your loser bunk is supposed to contaminate our bunk by touching it," Gaby said. She looked meaningfully at Grace's hand on the porch railing. Her bunkmates laughed.

"Oh. Sorry." Grace picked her hand up and tried to smile. Gaby was just kidding, she was pretty sure. It didn't sound like she was kidding, exactly, but she must be. The bunk rivalry wasn't a serious thing, after all. And besides, Gaby was her friend. Gaby was the one who'd wanted to be partners in drama and again in free swim. So she had to be kidding. She wasn't really being as mean as she sounded. Right?

"Um, I was wondering if you want to hang out," Grace said. "I'm not in the mood to stay in the bunk."

"Who could blame you? I bet it smells in there," Gaby said. Her bunkmates laughed again, and Gaby looked pleased. "But I *am* in the mood to stay in my bunk, and obviously you can't come in here," she went on.

"I . . . I can't?" Grace didn't know what else to say.

"No. How do we know you're not spying on us to help your bunk pull a prank?" Gaby said. "Everybody knows Jenna Bloom wants to prank us."

"Jenna's not planning any more pranks," Grace said honestly. "I think she's retired."

"Whatever. I'm not interested." Gaby stepped back inside and let the door swing shut in Grace's face.

Grace blinked at the dusty screen. Had her new best friend just slammed the door on her? Was this all some sort of joke that she didn't get? Was she supposed to follow Gaby inside?

She didn't think so. But then what *was* she supposed to do? She couldn't keep standing around outside by herself. "Okay. I'll see you later," she called through the screen door. Then she turned and stepped off the porch. She walked off toward the activities shacks as fast as she could. She had no idea what she'd do once she got there. All she knew was that she wanted to get as far away from Gaby as possible. And it looked like Gaby felt the same way about her!

chapter
SIX

At free swim, Grace put the tiny nose clip across the bridge of her nose and headed straight for the water. A good swim would relax her—and she needed to relax after the weird day she'd been having. First the letter from her mom, then Gaby's brush-off at 3A! She was totally stressed.

"Gracie, hey!" Gaby called, running up behind her. "Are you going in?"

Grace stopped, surprised. An hour ago, Gaby had been totally mean to her. But now she stood there with a big happy grin on her face, as if nothing had happened. *Maybe she really was playing around before,* Grace thought, confused. It didn't matter, though. Gaby had completely humiliated her in front of all of 3A. Grace wasn't in the mood for any more of Gaby's strange behavior.

"Um, yeah, I really want to swim some laps," Grace said. She tried to step around Gaby without seeming too rude. Sarah and Valerie were already in the water, and if she swam out to them, she knew they'd let her triple with them.

"I was thinking we could just hang out on

shore," Gaby said. "You know, put our feet in the water to cool off when we need to. It'll be fun. We can work on your audition scene."

Grace couldn't believe it. Gaby was just assuming they were going to be swim buddies again! Yesterday it had seemed like a good thing that Gaby thought they were close enough friends for that. But after the way she'd acted earlier today, Grace wasn't so sure anymore.

"I don't know," she said. "I was looking forward to swimming. And I don't think I'm going to audition."

Gaby frowned. But before she could say anything, Julie walked up. "Hey, guys," she said. "Grace, I need to borrow you for a minute."

"Okay." Normally Grace would be worried if Julie asked for a private conversation. But right now it was a relief to get away from Gaby. She was just too hard to figure out.

Grace followed Julie over to the canoe stands, where there were no campers. Her feet felt like lead as she tromped through the sand. She knew what was coming, and it wasn't going to be fun.

"Grace, you know I have to ask about your reading," Julie said.

"Yeah."

"How far have you gotten in *Call of the Wild?*"

Grace tried to remember what page she was on. She couldn't. "Far enough to know that I wouldn't want to be that dog," she said, hoping Julie would take that as a joke. The book was about a dog that, as far as she could tell, was in for a really bad life up in Alaska or someplace like that.

Julie didn't smile. "How many chapters have you read?"

"I'm not sure," Grace said. "A few. I think."

"How many is that?"

"Maybe three," Grace told her. "Well, I think I'm almost to chapter three."

Julie's face fell, and Grace looked down at her feet. She loved Julie—Julie was the coolest counselor at Lakeview! The last thing Grace wanted to do was disappoint her, but obviously she already had.

"Oh, Grace, what am I going to do with you?" Julie sighed. "You know I hate acting like a police officer. Why won't you just read the book?"

"It's boring," Grace said. "Every time I start reading it, I practically fall asleep. I'd rather be doing something fun with my friends."

"But you have to read it! You know you won't be able to go to the water park next week unless you finish it," Julie cried.

"I know." Grace kicked at the sand, frustrated. "But I don't even care about the stupid water park. All I care about is auditioning for the play, and I won't be able to do that, either!"

Tears filled her eyes. She'd managed to keep herself from thinking about this for a long time, but now that it was out there, all her emotions came rushing at her.

"Grace . . ." Julie reached out for her arm, but Grace pulled away. It was bad enough that she'd made Julie angry with her—she wasn't going to cry in front of her, too. She turned and ran toward the trees, her vision blurring.

As she passed the last of the canoes, Grace noticed Gaby standing behind it. Her supposed friend looked away quickly, but Grace got the feeling that she'd been hiding there for a while. Which meant that Gaby had heard the whole conversation with Julie.

Gaby knew everything, whether Grace wanted her to or not.

▲ ▲ ▲

"Look at that mop," Natalie teased as Grace shook the water out of her curly hair.

Grace jumped closer to her and shook herself like a dog, spraying water all over Natalie's face. Then she looked up innocently and said, "What? I didn't hear what you said, Natalie."

Natalie laughed and flicked her wet towel lightly at Grace.

"Hey, break it up," Alyssa joked. "No fighting between swim buddies."

Grace pulled her mass of hair back and wrangled it into a ponytail. She knew it wouldn't dry for the rest of the day, but it was worth the messy hair just to get in some swim time. After talking to Julie, she'd managed to calm herself down in the girls' room in time to squeeze in a few laps during free swim, with Nat and Alyssa as her partners. Gaby hadn't come near her since Grace caught her by the canoes, and Grace hoped it stayed that way. She didn't like to think that Gaby was eavesdropping, but there was no other reason for the girl to be hanging out nearby during a private talk.

"Let's get back fast," Natalie said, draping one arm over Grace's shoulders and the other over Alyssa's. "I hate sitting around in a wet suit. I want to be one of the first in the bathroom to change."

They started up the trail that led to the bunks.

"Only a few more days until the water park," Natalie

said, bouncing a little as she walked. "I can't wait!"

"Me neither." Alyssa leaned forward so she could see Grace on the other side of Natalie. "We forgot to ask you if you want to sit with us, Grace."

"Oh, yeah," Natalie put in. "Alex says they rent a school bus, so we can all squish into a three-seater."

"Definitely," Grace said. She loved hanging out with Natalie and Alyssa. They were always friendly and never made her feel like a third wheel. "You guys have never been on a camp field trip, huh?" she said.

"Not yet. This will be the first, not to mention the greatest," Alyssa said. "I love water parks."

"Cool, so we're all sitting together," Nat said. She squealed with excitement. "I can't wait!"

"I can't believe you," said a voice from behind them. Surprised, Grace turned to see Gaby following right on their heels.

"Me?" Grace said. "Why? What do you mean?"

"You're supposed to sit with me on the field-trip bus," Gaby said. "Obviously."

"I am?" Grace asked. "Since when? We never even talked about sitting together. I don't think we ever talked about the field trip at all."

"We're friends, aren't we?" Gaby snapped. "Friends sit together. I didn't know I had to make some elaborate plan about it."

Natalie and Alyssa stepped in closer to Grace, but they didn't say anything. Truthfully, she kind of wished they would—because she had no idea what to say herself. "How am I supposed to know if we're friends or not?" she sputtered. "You wouldn't even let me in your bunk. You were really mean."

Gaby rolled her eyes. "Don't be such a baby," she said. "I was only kidding."

"Oh." Grace felt stupid. Clearly she should've been able to tell that Gaby was joking around at bunk 3A, but it really hadn't seemed that way. "Well, sorry."

"Whatever," Gaby said. "So we'll sit together on the way to the water park?"

Grace bit her lip. She didn't really want to sit with Gaby. In fact, she wasn't sure she wanted to be friends with Gaby at all, let alone *best* friends. It was just too hard to figure out Gaby's behavior, and Grace never felt comfortable around her.

"No, I think I'm still going to sit with Nat and Alyssa on the field trip," she answered slowly. "They asked me first."

Gaby's face turned the same bright-orange shade as Alyssa's hair. Without thinking, Grace took a step back.

"I think she's gonna blow," Alyssa whispered.

"You're a rotten friend!" Gaby exploded, yelling right in Grace's face. "And I don't even care because you probably can't go on the field trip anyway!"

I knew it! Grace thought, horrified. *I knew she was eavesdropping on my talk with Julie!*

"You heard me," Gaby said to Natalie and Alyssa. "She told you she could sit with you, but she's lying. She's not even gonna be there."

"What are you talking about?" Natalie demanded. "Of course she is."

"Grace isn't a liar," Alyssa put in.

"She is, too," Gaby said smugly. "If she doesn't finish reading her lame-o book, she can't go to the water park. And there's no way she can finish it because she's barely even to chapter three!"

Natalie's mouth fell open. Alyssa whirled around to look at Grace. "Is that true?" she asked.

Grace had never been so angry in her entire life! How dare Gaby listen in on a private conversation and then tell everyone Grace's business? How dare she make Grace's friends think she was a liar?

How dare she be such a bully?

"Grace?" Nat said.

Natalie's worried eyes were too much for Grace to take. How could she explain all this to her bunkmates? That she couldn't go to the water park with them, and she couldn't try out for the play . . . and no matter how hard she tried, she couldn't seem to finish that stupid book!

Tears blurred her eyes again, but this time they were tears of anger. She pushed past her friends and Gaby and stomped off toward the office.

Dear Mom and Dad,

I can't believe you're doing this to me! Why are you trying to ruin my life? Now everyone knows that I can't go to the water park. Or at least they will know soon. I'm not sure whether they'll be mad at me or feel sorry for me, but either way they're not going to act normal around me for the rest of the summer. It's humiliating. Why can't you just let me be normal and do the things everyone else gets to do? It isn't fair! I promise I'll finish the books. Just please, please, please let me go to the water park and try out for the play and be normal! I know you're mad at me, but PLEASE don't ruin my whole summer! I love acting so much, and you're taking it away. Please let me audition, and let me go to WetWorld—I'll read as many books as you want!

Grace hit Send and watched the e-mail disappear from the screen. Immediately she wished she could get it back. It wasn't going to help. It would probably just make her parents even angrier at her than they already were, and she couldn't blame them.

She'd barely been able to convince them to let her come to camp this summer—there was no way they were going to let her go on the field trip now that she hadn't held up her end of the bargain.

She stood up and made her way to the door of the camp office. "Thanks, Dr. Steve," she called.

The camp director looked up from his desk and blinked at her. "That didn't take very long, Grace," he said. "Usually you're here for at least fifteen minutes when you send updates to your parents."

"I know. This was a short message," she said. "Anyway, thanks again for letting me use the computer."

"No problem, Grace." He went back to his paperwork, and she pushed open the door and stepped out into the sunshine. It felt weird to thank him for the computer when she didn't want to use it at all. If not for her father's phone call to Kathleen demanding daily e-mail updates on her reading, Grace would have spent the summer happily ignoring her parents. She wouldn't even have known that Dr. Steve had a computer with Internet access that the campers could use. And she would have gone on the field trip and tried out for the play and been totally happy.

She caught up with her bunkmates outside the mess hall, where everyone was milling around as usual before dinner. They all turned to stare the instant she walked up.

"Since I have your attention, I'd like to make an announcement," Grace said. "I no longer have to do chores. You will all take turns doing my chores for me for the rest of the summer."

Everyone laughed.

"What? I mean it," Grace said, laughing along

with them.

"You wish," Alex told her.

"So where were you?" Chelsea asked. "You keep going off by yourself lately."

Natalie and Alyssa wouldn't meet her eyes. Obviously they'd told everyone about the scene between Gaby and Grace, and now they felt guilty. Grace sighed. They shouldn't have to feel bad when she was the one who hadn't been telling the truth.

"I've been keeping a secret from you guys," Grace said, sticking her hands in her shorts pockets. She hated having to be all serious with her friends. Friends were supposed to be the people you had fun with! "You know how I've been reading *Call of the Wild?*"

Everybody nodded.

"It's not for fun."

"Shocker," Jenna said. All the other girls cracked up, but Grace frowned.

"What do you mean?" she asked. "I could be reading for fun. Lots of people do that. Look at Alyssa!"

Alyssa snorted. "Thanks."

"Grace, Alyssa likes to read," Brynn pointed out. "You don't. All last summer, I never once saw you with a book in your hand."

"Me either," Alex agreed.

"All we mean is that obviously you're not reading that book because you want to," Jenna said. "If you actually *wanted* to read it, you'd be done with it by now. So what's the deal?"

This was it. Grace couldn't put off telling them for another second. She bit her lip, hard. Were they going to think she was a total loser? Were they going to laugh at her? "You guys all have reading in school, right?" she blurted. "We have it as a separate class."

"So do we," Natalie agreed. "Every day we go to a different teacher for reading."

"Yeah, well, I failed it." Grace forced herself to say the words. "I got an F."

"In reading?" Chelsea said incredulously. "What kind of idiot fails reading?"

Grace winced. That was exactly the reaction she'd been expecting, and it hurt even more than she'd thought it would.

"Chelsea!" Natalie hissed.

"Chelsea!" Candace cried.

"What?" Chelsea said. "Grace knows how to read—we've all seen her do it. So how could she fail? The only reason people fail reading is because they're dyslexic or something and they need more time for the tests."

Everyone looked at Grace.

"Um, nope, no learning disability," she said. "I just failed."

"What happened?" Alyssa asked gently.

"Nothing really," Grace admitted. "I don't love to read, as you obviously all noticed. And there was always something better to do—talk to my best friend, play video games, act in the school play . . ."

"And?" Jenna prompted.

"And so I was busy goofing off, and I never finished any of the books I was supposed to read," Grace said in a rush. "And they failed me."

"So what now?" Valerie asked.

"You mean after my parents considered locking me in my room with a pile of books until I'm in college? We made a deal. I promised to read the two books I didn't read for class, and they let me come to camp this summer."

"They thought about taking away camp?" Alex sounded faint at the very idea of it.

"Yeah." Grace shuddered just remembering how upset she'd been at the prospect of missing Lakeview this year. "It was the worst. My dad had totally made up his mind that I was going to stay home all summer and read. It took me two solid days of begging before he changed his mind."

"And he came up with that bargain?" Brynn asked.

Grace nodded. "I agreed that during the first session I'd read *Call of the Wild*, and during the second session I'd read *The Jungle Book*. So they let me come." She looked around at all her bunkmates. "You guys, I've never been so upset in my whole life," she whispered. "Can you imagine if they took camp away?"

"But the first session is over," Karen said, horrified. "And you're still not done with *Call of the Wild*."

"That's why on Visiting Day I didn't have as much fun with my folks as any of you had with yours," Grace replied. "My father almost had a cow. He wanted to drag me back home that second."

"Oh, no," Brynn said. "So what happened?"

"They called Kathleen the other day to find out how I was doing with the book. That's when she and Julie called me aside. They made me go call my parents and tell them what page I was on."

"I knew it! I knew you were getting in trouble that day!" Chelsea cried triumphantly.

"Chelsea, don't," Karen said.

Everybody held their breath. Karen *never* corrected

Chelsea. How would Chelsea handle it?

"Excuse me? Don't *what?*" Chelsea demanded, turning on Karen.

"It's just . . . you're just . . ." Karen stammered. She looked terrified. "Never mind."

"So what happened when you called your parents, Grace?" Sarah asked, trying to draw attention away from poor Karen.

Grace winced just remembering that awful conversation. "My dad said I couldn't do the field trip or try out for the play until I'd finished *Call of the Wild.* And for this past week, they've been making me go to the office and e-mail them mini book reports so they'll know I'm reading it."

"But you haven't been reading it," Valerie said.

Has everyone been watching me? Grace wondered ruefully. *It's not just Julie. All the girls in the bunk seem to know how much I hate reading!* "I know," she said aloud. "I'm doomed."

"No you're not," Jenna said. "You're just being a flake."

Grace's mouth dropped open. She hadn't been expecting that. All she could think to do was laugh. "Excuse me?" she said.

"It's totally simple," Jenna went on. "Stop fooling around and read the book so you can come to the water park with us."

"Yeah," Alyssa put in. "Just read it. We don't want to leave you here all alone while we're at WetWorld."

"Especially not since you had to have such a fight just to sit with us on the bus," Nat added.

"I know!" Grace cried. "I can't believe Gaby told on me! She listened in on a private conversation between me and Julie."

"Well, you can't trust a girl from 3A," Brynn sniffed. "Anyway, you shouldn't have been keeping this a secret. It's no big deal."

Grace gazed around at the faces of her friends. They all looked concerned. Not one of them seemed about to tease her. Not even Chelsea. "I thought you guys would make fun of me," she said.

"For failing a class?" Alyssa asked. "Why would we make fun of that?"

"Yeah. That's not funny," Candace agreed.

"It's kind of embarrassing," Grace said.

Jenna snorted. "You can't be embarrassed in front of *us*. We're a team."

"You're right," Grace said, feeling better than she had all week. "I should have told you guys."

"That's right," Natalie said. "Believe me, I know how bad it is to keep secrets from your friends. Don't you feel better now?"

"Yeah," Grace said honestly. "I really do. But I don't think it's so simple. I'm not just behind on one book—now I'm behind on *two*! There's no way I'm going to make it to WetWorld."

Dear Grace,

It took a lot of convincing, but I finally managed to get your father to give you one last chance. You know neither of us want you to be unhappy, sweetheart. We know how important it is to feel "normal," and we know how important the camp play is to you. But you made a deal at the start of the summer,

and you haven't stuck to it. And reading is very important, honey. You're too smart to sell yourself short by failing a class that you should be able to pass. So Dad and I propose that you take a little quiz. Finish your first book by Sunday, and we'll e-mail you a list of questions about it. If you answer them ALL correctly, you can try out for the play on Wednesday . . . and go on the field trip on Thursday. We know you can do it, Grace. You're a very smart girl when you put your mind to something. It's up to you.
Love,
Mom
P.S. and Love, Dad too!

Grace's heart beat faster as she read the e-mail from her parents later that night. Kathleen had pulled her away before dessert to tell her that she had a message. Grace had been half expecting them to order her to pack her bags and come home, but instead, her mom was being nice about it. Grace felt a little pang of guilt. She knew her parents weren't trying to be mean by telling her she had to skip WetWorld. She hadn't given them any other choice. She hit Reply and typed in her own message:

Dear Mom (and Dad),
Thank you! Thank you! You're the best parents in the world! I know it's my last chance, and I'm not going to do anything else between now and Monday except read my book.
Love,
Grace

She hit Send, closed out of her e-mail account, and headed out of the office, skipping down the few steps leading to the main trail. Maybe she could go to WetWorld after all. And best of all, maybe she could try out for the play!

But she still had to finish that whole long book first, and she only had three days to do it. Grace's steps slowed as she thought about *The Call of the Wild*. She knew her parents were being super nice to her and really giving her a second chance. But so far she hadn't even been able to deal with having homework over the summer.

How was she supposed to handle such an important quiz?

chapter
EIGHT

Grace was awake and reading before the bugle the next morning. She didn't want to be, but now that there was a chance she could audition for the play, she knew she had to do her absolute best to finish the book.

She read through breakfast. She read on the walk to the mess hall and back, with Natalie and Alyssa holding her arms, steering her down the path. After Candace offered to take over her chores so Grace could finish the book, she read while everyone else was working. But soon enough it was time for their first free choice. Grace reluctantly put down her book. She was almost to chapter five.

"Ready for arts and crafts?" Julie asked, giving Grace's ponytail an affectionate tug.

"Not really," Grace admitted. "I feel like if I put my book down even for an hour, I won't be able to finish it on time."

"Are you liking it any better?" Julie asked.

Grace thought about it. She'd been so busy trying to speed-read the book that she hadn't paid much attention to what she thought about the story.

"I guess I am," she said, surprised. "Everyone is being so mean to the poor dog, I want to know how he triumphs at the end."

Julie grinned. "That's what I like to hear. Reading is supposed to be fun, you know."

"It would be more fun if I could act it out," Grace joked. "Although I don't know how I'd play a dog."

"I'll tell you what, my little actress," Julie said. "I'll let you skip arts and crafts today as long as you stay in the bunk and read."

"Really? You rule!" Grace bounced up and down in happiness. "I don't have to skip drama too, though, do I?" she asked.

"No way," Julie said. "I know what your priorities are."

"I just love it," Grace admitted.

"I know. You never take a long time to read scenes that you're doing in class," Julie said. "So obviously you can read fast when you want."

"I'm reading the book fast now, too." Grace jumped back onto her bunk and pulled out *The Call of the Wild*.

"Okay. I'll be back in fifteen minutes," Julie said. "I have a quick meeting with Kathleen and then I'll swing by art and crafts and tell Richie where you are."

"Mm-hmm," Grace said, already back in the world of Buck the dog.

She read straight through lunch and continued in the drama shack right until Bethany called them all to attention. Grace finally put the book away and looked around. Gaby was sitting as far from her as possible. And Devon was standing up in front of the class with Simon, Natalie's sort-of boyfriend.

"Okay, boys," Bethany said. "Show us the scene

you've been working on."

For the first time all day, Grace forgot about Buck and the Yukon. The two boys were acting out a scene from an old movie called *The Outsiders*. Simon's character was dying, and Devon's character, his best friend, was there by his side in the hospital.

Most of the kids who took drama at camp liked to goof around and play improv games. But Simon, and especially Devon, obviously took the class seriously. They were really acting. Even Brynn would approve. Grace found herself getting caught up in the lives of the two characters. She could swear she saw tears in Devon's eyes as he spoke to his best friend for the last time.

When the scene ended, she clapped so hard that her hands hurt. Devon shot her a smile and nodded to say thank you.

"Somebody liiikes you," Brynn said in a singsong voice, nudging Grace.

"No way," Grace said quickly. "He was just saying thanks for the applause. You know, from everyone. He was thanking everyone."

"Uh-huh," Brynn said sarcastically.

"He was really good in that scene," Grace added.

"Uh-huh," Brynn said again, wiggling her eyebrows.

"Oh, be quiet," Grace mumbled. "I just think he's a good actor." *And a cute one*, she added silently. She didn't usually like boys, but she wouldn't mind doing a scene with him.

When Grace got back to the bunk, she was surprised to hear voices coming from inside. Everyone else was supposed to be at a camp-wide nature meeting. Dr. Steve had gotten an environmental conservationist to come and teach them about endangered species. Grace thought it sounded interesting, but reading was more important right now. She'd gotten permission to go back to the bunk so she could spend her time with Buck in *The Call of the Wild*.

But somebody else was clearly there.

Grace was about to open the door when she heard Chelsea raise her voice. "Because I said so!" she was saying. She sounded angry.

Grace hesitated. Maybe she shouldn't interrupt.

"But, Chelsea, I love water parks," Karen's quiet voice drifted out. "The most fun I ever had was at a water park when I was eight."

"Have you ever seen what people look like when they go on those rides?" Chelsea argued. "Your hair gets all flat and stringy, and your makeup washes all off."

"I never noticed that," Karen replied.

And why does it matter? Grace wondered. Should she go in there? Part of her wanted to rush in and help Karen deal with Chelsea. But those two were best friends, after all. They seemed to be having an argument, and Grace didn't think she should stick her nose in their business.

"Well, it's true. We'd look horrible if we went on all those rides."

"But it would be fun." Karen sounded wistful. Grace was surprised Karen was disagreeing with Chelsea at all— Karen must really love those water rides if she was willing to fight for them.

Suddenly Chelsea gave a little sob. It sounded fake. "I can't believe you're changing your mind about this," she said. "You promised to hang out with me by the wave pool."

"I know," Karen said. "Don't be mad—"

"You know that swimming makes me sick," Chelsea interrupted. "If we go on those rides, I'll get water in my ears and get an earache. And if water gets in my eyes, it will ruin my contact lenses."

But you go swimming in the lake every day, Grace thought.

"But we go swimming every day," Karen said.

"Yeah, in the lake," Chelsea answered. Her voice wavered as if she were trying to hold back tears. "Where there's no chlorine to sting my eyes. And where I can keep my head out of the water so my hair doesn't get ruined. And I don't get water in my ears."

Grace shook her head. Chelsea was coming up with all kinds of excuses, but Grace suspected that the real reason she didn't want to go on the water rides was that she thought she'd look bad with wet hair and no makeup. Chelsea was so pretty that she'd be gorgeous no matter what. But she took a lot of care with her appearance. Maybe she didn't feel confident without her makeup.

Still, it wasn't fair to keep Karen from doing what she wanted just because Chelsea didn't want to be alone. *Tell her that, Karen,* Grace silently willed. *Tell her you want to go on the rides.*

"Well, if it means that much to you . . ." Karen said.

"Thank you!" Chelsea answered, her voice normal again. "We'll have a great time getting a tan."

"I usually just get sunburns," Karen replied quietly.

Grace took a deep breath and opened the door. "Oh, hi, guys," she said casually. "I didn't know anyone was in here."

Chelsea looked startled. Karen just smiled. "We came back to get Chelsea's sunglasses," she explained. "The light hurts her eyes."

"Plus, who wants to listen to a boring lecture?" Chelsea added, trying to joke. She watched Grace carefully, as if waiting for her to say something. *She wants to know if I overheard them arguing about the water park,* Grace realized.

But she had no intention of saying anything about what she'd heard. She wasn't happy that Karen had given in to Chelsea, but it wasn't really any of her business.

"Julie said I could skip the lecture so I can read," she said, flopping down on her bed.

"We better get back before Julie comes looking for us," Karen told Chelsea.

"Yeah. See you later, Grace."

Grace smiled and waved as they left. It was hard to understand Chelsea sometimes. But right now she had to focus on her book.

🔺 🔺 🔺

"Hey, Grace, your *friend* is here." Valerie's tone was sarcastic.

Grace looked up from her book. She'd been reading in the bunk for an hour and a half straight. "Huh?"

Valerie nodded toward the porch. "That girl from 3A. Abby?"

"Gaby," Grace corrected her. "She's here?"

"On the porch. I guess she didn't feel like taking

siesta with her own bunkmates," Valerie said.

"I guess I can't avoid her, huh?" Grace murmured. "Did you tell her I was here?"

"Well, I wasn't gonna lie," Valerie said. "Just go out and talk to her. The sooner you get rid of her, the sooner you can get back to reading."

"Yeah," Candace said. "The sooner you can get back to reading so you can come to WetWorld."

"Oh, all right." Grace got up and went out onto the porch. She wasn't in the mood for small talk, but she figured Gaby must have a reason for coming here. She probably wanted to apologize for telling Natalie and Alyssa about Grace's secret. "Hey, what's up?" she said when she reached Gaby.

"Hi, Gracie!" Gaby chirped. "Wanna hang out?"

"I can't," Grace said. "I have to read."

Gaby frowned. "Is this because I wouldn't hang out with you during siesta the other day?"

"No," Grace said honestly. "Although it is a little weird that you feel comfortable coming over to my bunk when you told me to stay away from your bunk."

"I told you I was just kidding about that."

"Yeah, I know," Grace said. "It still seems a little weird to me, though. And it sure didn't sound like you were kidding. Anyway, I really have to read."

"Look, I'm sorry," Gaby blurted out. "I shouldn't have told your bunkmates that you lied about WetWorld."

It didn't seem like much of an apology, but still Grace felt a little better. At least Gaby realized that what she'd done was rude and wrong. "That's okay," Grace said. "I might get to go to WetWorld after all."

"Cool," Gaby said. "How?"

"I have to finish this book by the end of the weekend," Grace explained. "And then my parents are going to give me a quiz. That's why I can't hang out right now. I have a lot of reading to do."

"Okay. How about at free swim? Do you want to be swim buddies? It's so hot out, I'm dying to go in the lake."

"Um, I don't think so," Grace said. "I was planning to read during free swim. Julie even let me get out of arts and crafts this morning so I could read."

"Then you don't have to read during free swim," Gaby said. "Give yourself a break. Get some exercise."

"But I can't," Grace insisted. "There's no way I can finish the book unless I spend every single second reading."

"Oh, come on, don't be so boring," Gaby said. "I thought you were supposed to be fun."

"I *am* fun," Grace replied. "Just not right now. Being too much fun is what got me into this mess. If I'd paid more attention to school and spent less time having fun, I wouldn't have to be cooped up in here reading all day."

"It's only one hour," Gaby pointed out. "And we just made up after our fight. Please?"

Grace sighed. How could she say no to that?

"Okay," she said. "I guess I can take one hour off from reading."

Once Gaby had gone back to her own bunk, Grace managed to finish the chapter she was on and start the next one before it was time for free swim. Changing into her bathing suit, she decided Gaby was right. She'd been reading nonstop for hours. She could use a break.

It was hot out, with no wind. The lake barely even

had ripples on its surface. Perfect for swimming laps, which Grace couldn't wait to do. When she got in the water, she knew her stress about the quiz on Sunday would start to melt away. She'd cool down, enjoy the feel of the water against her skin, and clear her mind from the adventures of Buck for a little while. She couldn't wait to get into the lake. She put her swimming clip on her nose and looked around for Gaby.

Grace found her sitting on a towel near the shallow part of the lake. "Hey!" Grace called, walking over. "Ready to swim?"

"Oh, I don't want to swim," Gaby said, squinting up at Grace. "I figured we'd sunbathe."

Grace almost laughed. She and Gaby were two of the palest, most freckled kids at camp. Neither one of them was ever going to get a tan—all sunbathing would do was burn them to a crisp or leave them with twice as many freckles. "I'd rather swim," Grace said. "If we were just going to lie in the sun, I would've brought my book."

"I would've brought my book," Gaby repeated in a high-pitched imitation of Grace. "Can't you talk about anything but that dumb book?" she added.

"I have to finish it," Grace cried. "I told you that! You said you wanted to swim."

Gaby heaved a huge sigh. "Oh, all right," she said as if she were doing Grace a big favor. "Let's go in."

"Cool." Grace turned and started toward the deeper section where they could swim laps.

"Let's just go in over here," Gaby called behind her. "Like we did the other day."

Grace glanced back, surprised to find Gaby standing near the shallow end where all the little kids swam. "Why?" she asked. "We can't really swim there. It only comes up to our waists."

"We don't have to *swim* swim," Gaby said. "We can just splash around and get cooled off."

"But I want to swim laps," Grace said. She tried to remember whether she'd ever seen Gaby swimming in the lake. "Aren't you a green yet?" she asked. Maybe Gaby hadn't learned to dive this summer, in which case she'd still be in the yellow group of swimmers. They weren't allowed to go in the deep part during free swim.

Gaby snorted. "Please. I'm a blue already."

Now Grace was really confused. If Gaby was in the blue group, it meant she was an expert swimmer who'd already passed her swimming safety test. So why didn't she want to go in the deep section? "Well, come on then," Grace said. "Let's go swim."

"But our towels and stuff are over here," Gaby argued. "I don't want to have to walk all the way back from the deep part to get a towel."

"It's a hundred degrees out!" Grace pointed out. "It's not like you'll be cold walking ten feet farther."

"I'm not in the mood to swim," Gaby said. "My contact lenses are bothering me."

"Oh. I didn't know you wore contacts."

"Yeah, and I can't put my face in the water with them in," Gaby said. "So I can't really swim. All I can do is go in over here where I can keep my head out."

Grace frowned. "Then how did you pass your test to be a blue?"

"I wore my glasses that day and took them off to swim. Are we done with the third degree?" Gaby said. "Come on." Without waiting, she walked into the water in the shallow section.

Frustrated, Grace pulled off her nose clip and followed. Wading around in muddy water wasn't exactly her idea of a good time. She was annoyed at Gaby, but she was even madder at herself. No matter how hard she tried, she just didn't seem able to say no to Gaby.

Walking around in the shallow water was boring, so they only stayed in the lake for ten minutes. Then Grace had to sit on shore and listen to Gaby tell gossipy stories about her bunkmates until free swim was over. Grace had never been so happy to hear Tyler blow his whistle.

"Everybody out!" he yelled. "See you tomorrow!"

"Okay, bye," Grace said in a rush, gathering up her towel.

"What's the hurry?" Gaby asked.

"I have to go read."

"Well, hang on, I'll walk with you." Gaby slowly picked up her towel, shook it out, and folded it neatly. Grace bounced from one foot to the other in impatience. Finally Gaby was ready to go.

"Should we catch up to Marta and Sharon?" Grace asked, spotting two of Gaby's bunkmates on the path ahead of them.

"Nah." Something in Gaby's voice made Grace suspicious. She looked around. None of the other girls from 3A were anywhere near them. In fact, none of Gaby's bunkmates were ever around. It didn't seem as if Gaby hung out with them at all away from the bunk. And based on her nasty stories during free swim, Gaby didn't seem to mind.

"So who's your best friend in the bunk?" Grace asked.

Gaby shrugged. "No one. It's better to have a best friend from outside the bunk."

Grace didn't answer. She'd given up on thinking that Gaby could be her best friend at camp. Gaby was too unpredictable to count on. One minute she was nice, and the next she was mean.

"Oh, hang on," Gaby said suddenly. "I have to fix my shoe." She dropped to her knees and began fiddling with the Velcro on her sandals. But Grace noticed that there was nothing wrong with the shoe to begin with. Gaby had just pulled it open and then started playing around with it. Was she trying to hide from someone? The only people on the path behind them were Julie and Lizzie, Gaby's counselor. All the other campers were way up ahead.

Julie and Lizzie stepped around them and kept walking. The second they were gone, Gaby popped back up. "Okay, let's go," she said cheerfully.

But Grace didn't buy it. Gaby had been trying to avoid Julie and Lizzie—she was sure of it. "Hey, Julie!" she called without warning Gaby. "Wait up!"

Julie and Lizzie turned around and waited for them.

"What'd you do that for?" Gaby whispered. Grace ignored her and hurried to catch up to the counselors.

"Hey, Grace, I was surprised to see you without your book," Julie said. "Are you finished with it?"

Gaby snorted. "Yeah, right. With how slow she reads?"

Grace felt a wave of anger wash through her body. How would Gaby know how fast or slow she read?

"Don't be nasty, Gaby," Lizzie said seriously. "You

finally finished your week in the yellow zone. Do you want to make it another week?"

Gaby shot Grace an angry look. "Sorry," she said, not sounding sorry at all.

Grace waited until they'd reached the bunk area before pulling Gaby aside. "What did Lizzie mean back there?" she demanded. "She said you had a week in the yellow zone."

Gaby rolled her eyes. "Oh, my stupid bunkmate Christa went whining to Lizzie about me using up her shampoo. So I got in trouble. Christa's such a baby."

A hard knot formed in Grace's stomach. "You were being punished?" she said angrily. "You had to stay in the shallow part of the lake with the yellows?"

"Yeah, can you believe that?" Gaby said. "No swimming in the deep end for a week! Just because I borrowed some shampoo."

Grace had a feeling that Gaby hadn't borrowed anything. Christa was a shy girl in 3A. She'd always reminded Grace of Karen. And knowing their two personalities, Grace thought Gaby had probably just used up Christa's shampoo and expected her not to tell. But that wasn't what bothered Grace most.

"You mean, all week you've tried to keep me from swimming in the deep part just so you would have company while you were being punished?" she asked.

"Well, I didn't want to hang out with the little kids all by myself," Gaby said.

"They're not all little," Grace pointed out. "Some of them just aren't strong swimmers yet."

"Still," Gaby said. "I'm not friends with any yellows."

"Why didn't you just ask me to stay in the shallow part with you?" Grace said, exasperated. "If you'd asked me as a friend, I would've been happy to do it for you."

"What's the difference?" Gaby said.

"You've been lying all week!" Grace cried.

Gaby shook her head. "You should talk. You lied to your bunkmates about the field trip."

"Well, I shouldn't have," Grace retorted. But Gaby was already walking away.

Grace turned toward her bunk with a heavy heart. She clearly wasn't going to be friends with Gaby at all: She hadn't had any fun during free swim, and worst of all, she'd missed an hour's worth of reading time!

chapter

"Hang on a minute, Grace," Julie said as Grace reached for the door of bunk 3C. Julie and Marissa were sitting on the rickety railing around the porch. "We need to talk to you."

Uh-oh, Grace thought. If there was one thing she'd learned in a summer and a half at camp, it was that when both the counselor and the CIT wanted to have a talk with you, it meant you were in trouble. But what could she possibly have done in the five minutes since she last saw Julie on the trail?

She followed them over to the picnic table and sat down.

"Grace, your parents called during free swim," Marissa said. "I had to tell them you couldn't come to the phone because you were busy swimming."

"Oh, no." Grace dropped her head onto the wooden table. "And they were mad that I wasn't reading."

"Yes," Marissa said. "Although I told them that you'd been reading all day, and that I didn't think there was any harm in taking one hour off to let your eyes rest."

"Thanks," Grace mumbled without lifting her head.

"But that's not what we're worried about," Julie said. "You really buckled down and worked today, Grace. So why did you decide not to read during free swim?"

"Gaby talked me into being her swim buddy," Grace said, looking up at them. "I figured doing a few laps might wake me up a little so that I could read all night tonight. But then we spent all our time in the shallow end, so I didn't even get to do laps." Grace sighed. "Believe it or not, I would rather have been reading."

Julie chuckled. "That's a new Grace, all right."

"Didn't Gaby tell you that she had to stay in the shallow part when she asked you to be her swim buddy?" Marissa asked. "Stephanie told me a week ago that Gaby was being punished." Jenna's sister Stephanie was the CIT for Gaby's bunk.

"Nope." All of Grace's annoyance crept back into her voice as she spoke. "She didn't bother to mention that until *after* free swim."

Julie and Marissa exchanged a glance. "How come you agreed to be swim buddies, Grace?" Julie asked. "I don't mean to sound harsh, but it doesn't sound as if you even like Gaby that much."

"I don't know," Grace said. "She's weird, but it's nice having a friend at camp."

"You have a million friends," Marissa cried. "Everybody loves you, Grace!"

"Yeah, I know. But I don't have a best friend," Grace said. "Everybody pairs off, but not with me. I guess I thought it would be cool to have one best friend here."

"It's okay to have a lot of friends," Marissa said. "It doesn't mean there's anything wrong with you if you don't have a best friend, you know. It just proves that you're well-rounded!"

"But I miss my best friend from home," Grace said with a sigh. "If she even is my best friend anymore. I owe her a letter, big time."

"You miss your best friend, so you thought you'd feel better if you found a best friend here," Julie said. "And you thought that Gaby was that friend?"

Grace frowned. "At first I thought she was cool, but then she started being mean a lot. Still, every time I try to disagree with her, it's like she turns my words around or something."

"Do you want me to have a talk with Lizzie about it?" Julie asked.

"No!" Grace cried. "It's totally fine. I can handle her."

"You sure?" Marissa asked. "We're here to help if you need us."

"Thanks, but no. Gaby's fine. I'm just mad at myself because I knew I should be reading during swim." Grace stood up. "In fact, I'm not putting that book down again until I'm finished."

She gave them a little wave and headed for the bunk, her heart beating fast. She hoped she'd convinced them not to talk to Lizzie. The last thing she needed was Gaby to think she'd snitched on her. She knew Julie and Marissa meant well, but she also knew that campers weren't supposed to complain about other campers. It just wasn't cool. From now on, she'd simply stay away from Gaby. If she didn't have a best friend, then she could just take care of herself.

"Mind if I join you?" Natalie asked. She held up a romance novel. "Shove over."

Grace grinned at her and moved over on the old park bench. She'd come to the clearing around the flagpole to get in some quiet reading before dinner. Sarah and Valerie had promised to come get her on the way to the mess hall.

"My book is more fun than yours," Natalie said apologetically.

The cover showed two teenagers holding hands and looking all gooey and in love. Grace wrinkled her nose. "I don't think so," she said. "I'd rather read about a noble dog than read some stupid love story."

Natalie shook her head. "I don't know what's wrong with all you guys," she said. "I can't believe I'm stuck in a bunk with so many boy-haters."

"I don't hate boys," Grace said. "I just don't *like* them."

"You're hopeless." Nat opened her book, and Grace went back to reading *The Call of the Wild*. As the minutes passed, the late-afternoon sun; the thick, hot air; and the buzz of cicadas in the trees all drifted away from her mind as she lost herself in the story. She was so focused on it that she didn't even hear anyone approach until Natalie started talking.

Grace looked up and jumped in surprise. Simon and Devon stood two feet away, and she hadn't even known they were there. Simon and Natalie were discussing the WetWorld trip. And Devon was watching Grace. Immediately her cheeks grew hot. Why was he staring at her that way? How long had he been there?

He reached out toward her. Instinctively, Grace

pulled away, dropping her book. But before she could grab it, Devon bent and picked it up. "I love this book," he said, handing it back.

"Oh." Grace couldn't think of a single thing to say to that. *I'm only reading it because my parents are forcing me to* didn't seem like the correct response.

"Did you get to the part where he pulls the thousand-pound sled yet?"

"I'm in the middle of that right now," Grace said. "Don't tell me how it ends." She could hardly believe it herself, but she was dying to know whether Buck made it back to his master with the sled. His master had bet a lot of money, and Buck really wanted to win it for him.

"We got a puppy last year, and I made my parents name him Buck after this dog," Devon said.
"Wow. You really *do* love this book," she replied. He blushed a little, which only made him look cuter. Grace couldn't believe she thought he was cute. *He's gross*, she told herself. *All boys are gross.*

"It's cool that you like to read," he said. "It really helps with acting. You know that scene we did the other day? That's from a movie based on a book."

"It is?" Grace asked in surprise.

Simon groaned. "Believe it. Devon made me read the scene from the book *and* memorize the lines from the movie." He glanced at Natalie. "Drama is turning into a tough class, not just your average fun and easy free choice."

"It's all these actors," Natalie joked, her eyes shining as she nudged Grace with her arm. "They take everything so seriously."

"Didn't reading the book help you understand the

characters better?" Devon challenged.

"I hate to say it, but yes," Simon replied.

"See?" Devon winked at Grace. "It's good to be a book lover."

"Uh-huh." Once again, she couldn't think of anything to say. Since when was she at a loss for words? The other three were managing to have a perfectly normal conversation, and all she could do was sit there stupidly.

"See you at dinner," Simon told Natalie. She beamed back at him. "Okay."

"Later," Devon added.

"Uh-huh," Grace said again.

Natalie turned in her seat and stared at Grace until the boys left the clearing. Then she burst out laughing.

"What?" Grace said, pretending to ignore the laughter.

"That was priceless!" Natalie crowed.

"I don't know what you're talking about," Grace lied.

"I thought you didn't like boys," Nat giggled. "But maybe you don't like boys because you like just *one* boy."

"No way," Grace teased. "Simon is *your* boyfriend."

Natalie swatted her arm. "I mean Devon, and you know it."

"He's just a kid from my drama class."

"Mm-hmm," Natalie said, her eyebrows raised.

"And he's very talented," Grace added. "I appreciate his acting ability. That's all."

"Riiight," Nat replied sarcastically. "It has nothing to do with how cute he is."

"Is he cute? I hadn't noticed." Grace opened her

book and pretended to read, but she could tell Natalie was on to her. She did think Devon was cute. But so what? She acted like a dope around him, and that was no fun.

"Devon and Grace sitting in a tree," Natalie sang under her breath as she went back to her own book.

"Quit it," Grace said. But she knew it was hopeless. When Nat had first met Simon, everyone in the bunk had teased her constantly. It was only fair that she tease back.

"K-i-s-s-i-n-g," Natalie sang on.

"You're such a second-grader," Grace mumbled. Nat cracked up, and after a minute Grace did, too. Even though Natalie was making fun of her, there was nothing mean about it. And when Valerie and Sarah showed up to get them for dinner, Natalie didn't say a word about Devon and Grace. It was their secret.

▲ ▲ ▲

Grace was half asleep by the time everyone had brushed their teeth and gotten into bed that night. She'd never known that reading could be such hard work—she was exhausted!

Marissa took her place on her cot and started digging around in the milk crate she kept next to it. That was where she stored all her fashion magazines.

"Which magazine are you going to read us tonight?" Grace asked her. "I vote for *Cosmopolitan* horoscopes!"

But Marissa pulled out a spiral notebook, not a magazine. "I'm not reading tonight," she replied. "We have a surprise instead."

All around the bunk, the other girls were pulling out notebooks or pieces of paper. Jenna had a napkin with something scrawled on it in magic marker. "What's going on?" Grace asked, confused.

"We came up with a group assignment during chores this morning," Julie explained. "Everyone had to come up with one question about *Call of the Wild*, and tonight we're going to quiz you to help you study for your parents' quiz on Sunday. And then we'll do the same thing tomorrow night and Sunday morning."

"Are you kidding?" Grace asked. "You guys would do that for me?"

"It's no big deal," Chelsea said. "We all read the book in school."

"Yeah, but still," Grace protested. "You guys didn't mess up your grades. You shouldn't have to do schoolwork over the summer!"

"That's what friends are for," Sarah said.

"We have to make sure you can audition for the play," Brynn added. "How else could we keep our pact from last summer?"

"And besides, it's an excuse for a party," Jenna added. She pulled the box with the orange stickers out from under her bed. "My mom sent brownies!"

"We already brushed our teeth," Alex protested.

"So what? We can brush again later," Jenna said.

"Well, I don't like the taste of toothpaste with chocolate," Alex grumbled.

"Suit yourself," Jenna said. "You never want my mom's sweets, anyway."

"I want a brownie!" Grace put in.

"No way," Marissa said. "You have to earn your brownies, missy. Whenever you get a question right, you get a bite of brownie."

"I want to go first," Alyssa said.

"I'm next!" Valerie cried.

"Why don't we just go around the room," Julie suggested. "Marissa and I will go last."

Grace couldn't believe her luck. After spending half the week with Gaby, she'd forgotten how amazing real friends could be.

"What's the dog's name?" Alyssa asked.

Grace rolled her eyes. "That's too easy. His name is Buck."

Jenna tossed her a little piece of brownie.

"What's his master's name?" Sarah asked.

"Which one?" Grace replied. "He has a lot of masters over the course of the book."

Jenna gave a whistle. "Can't catch her with trick questions," she joked.

"List all of Buck's masters, then," Sarah said.

"Okay. Um, first there's the judge. And then there's François and Perrault. And John Thornton. And Hal and his family."

Jenna threw her another bite-size piece of brownie. "I feel like the dog," Grace joked. "Getting treats when I'm good!"

"Who wrote the book?" Valerie asked. "And when?"

"Jack London," Grace answered. "A long time ago."

Everybody laughed. "I'm going to write down the ones you don't know," Julie said. "That way we'll know what to focus on when we help you study tomorrow."

Grace looked around the room at all of her friends in their pj's, concentrating hard on a discussion about a book they'd all read ages ago. "You guys are the absolute nicest bunkmates in history," she said.

"Aw, you're so sweet," Natalie told her. "But that's

not going to make us go easy on you."

Grace grinned. "Okay. Give me the next question. I'm ready."

▲ ▲ ▲

"Just remember: WetWorld," Sarah said on Sunday. "Stay focused on that and you'll ace the test for sure."

Grace took a shaky breath. Her bunkmates had all decided to walk her to Dr. Steve's office to take her parents' quiz. Just having them there made her feel better, but her mouth still felt dry from nervousness. "What if I blank on everything?" she asked.

"You won't blank," Natalie said. "We've been quizzing you so much, you know everything there is to know about this book."

"And besides, I have a giant brownie with your name on it," Jenna added. "You finish the quiz, you get the whole thing!"

Grace smiled. "You saved me a brownie?"

"Yup. And it wasn't easy," Jenna joked.

They'd reached the office. Grace's heart did a flip-flop. Her parents would be so disappointed in her if she failed this quiz. Not to mention all the camp things that were riding on it—WetWorld, and most of all, the play.

"Okay. Wish me luck," Grace said.

"Good luck," bunk 3C yelled.

She stepped inside the office, where Kathleen was waiting for her. Kathleen nodded toward the computer. "It's all yours," she said. "Good luck, Grace."

"Thanks." Grace took a seat at the computer table. Her parents had sent a total of twenty questions about *The Call of the Wild*, which Kathleen had set up for her on the computer. She was supposed to answer all the questions and e-mail them back. Kathleen sat reading the newspaper at Dr. Steve's desk, acting as test monitor.

"WetWorld," Grace whispered. "And brownies." She took a deep breath and began the test.

1. What kind of dog is Buck?

Grace smiled. That one was easy. She typed in the answer: *a mix of Saint Bernard and Scottish shepherd.* Then for good measure, she decided to add a little more detail. *He's a noble dog who leads a pampered life in California until he's kidnapped and brought into the harsh wilderness of the Yukon.* She finished the sentence and sat back with a grin. She wished she could see her father's face when he read that one. He'd be so proud of her.

Grace took a deep breath and moved on to the next question. Remembering all the study questions her bunkmates had asked her over the weekend, she wasn't nervous at all.

2. Who is Buck's favorite master and why?

Grace knew that one. She'd talked about it with her friends, and it had led to a long conversation about everyone's relationships with their own dogs. She typed: *Buck's favorite master is John Thornton, and Buck loves him because Thornton has respect for Buck. Also, he saved Buck's life. And please give Mr. Fluffhead a kiss for me.*

Grace had named her dog Mr. Fluffhead even though he wasn't the least bit fluffy. He had short, coarse fur. But she was only five when she got him, and Mr. Fluffhead was the only name she could think of.

3. Name some of the other dogs on Buck's sled team.

Grace smiled. This was easy! She wrote down the

names of all the dogs on the team. And then she just kept going, answering the questions one after another without even pausing to think.

20. How much money does Buck win for John Thornton in the sled-pulling bet?

Immediately Jenna's face sprang into her mind. "I'd pull a heavy sled for that much money, too!" her friend had joked just last night. Grace quickly typed the answer: *$1,600.*

That's Devon's favorite part of the book, she thought. *I'll have to tell him that I finally finished it.* And even though she was sitting in Dr. Steve's office and Devon was nowhere in sight, she felt herself blush. *Stay focused!* she commanded herself.

She finished the whole quiz. Not one single question had stumped her. She read over her answers anyway, just to double-check. Then she crossed her fingers and hit Send.

"Well?" Kathleen asked. "How did you do?"

"I think I aced it," Grace reported. "My whole bunk helped me study all weekend."

"And they're going to help you celebrate if you pass," Kathleen said, gesturing out the office window. "They've been lined up out there for ten minutes."

"Really?" Grace ran over to the window and peered out. Her bunkmates sat in a row in front of the office shack. Nat and Alyssa were playing cat's cradle with some string. Chelsea was sunbathing. Candace, Karen, Jessie, and Sarah were all reading books. Valerie was asleep with her baseball cap over her face. Jenna and Alex tossed a mini soccer ball back and forth. And Brynn was talking to herself. Grace smiled. Obviously Brynn was practicing her lines for the play audition.

"You can head over to dinner now," Kathleen said. "Afterward, come back here to call your folks and see how you did."

"Okay," Grace said.

Kathleen tugged lightly on Grace's ponytail. "I'm proud of you, kiddo," she said. "A week ago, you couldn't have even finished half of those questions."

Grace nodded. "But I have to get them all right or else I can't go on the field trip."

"Try to relax and have fun at dinner," Kathleen said. "There's no point in worrying now."

But it was impossible to relax during dinner. All of Grace's bunkmates kept chattering about the trip to WetWorld. Grace knew they were trying to keep her mind off the quiz, but it wasn't working. The pork chops tasted even more like sawdust than usual. She could hardly wait for dinner to end. Her whole future at camp this summer depended on the results of this quiz. Would she get to go on the field trip? Would she have to start rehearsing an audition piece, too?

As soon as dinner was over, she sprinted back to the office and dialed her home number. "Mom?" she said as soon as she heard someone pick up.

"Hi, honey!" her mother replied. "I'm so proud of you!"

Grace took a huge gulp of air. She hadn't even realized she'd been holding her breath. "You are?" she asked. "Did I do okay?"

"Is that our brilliant daughter?" Her dad's voice came on the line. *He must've picked up the phone in the den,*

Grace thought.

"Hi, Daddy!" she said. "How did I do? Did I get them all right?"

"What do you think?" he asked.

Grace considered. All the questions had seemed pretty straightforward. None of them had given her any reason to doubt her answers. "I think I got them all," she said slowly. "They weren't hard."

"That's because you really read the book," her mother replied. "The questions would have seemed hard if you had just skimmed through the chapters without paying attention to what you were reading."

"You mean the way I usually do," Grace said.

"Well . . . yes. You're always more interested in whatever else is going on around you," her father answered. "But this time you obviously focused on what you were reading and took it in."

"Yeah, I did," Grace said. "I just tuned out everything else and read for hours."

"How did you like that?" her mom asked.

"Not as much as I like hanging out with my friends," Grace admitted. "But I did like the story. By the time I got halfway through, I really wanted to know what happened to Buck."

"That's good enough for now," her father said. "You got every question right, and we're happy."

"Does this mean I can go to WetWorld?" Grace asked. "And audition for the play?"

"Yes and yes," her mother replied. "As long as you start reading *The Jungle Book* right away."

"I will! I totally will this time," Grace promised. "I let you guys down once, and you gave me a second chance. I'm not going to let you down again."

"That's what I like to hear," her father said.

"Good night, honey. We're proud of you," her mother added.

When Grace hung up the phone, she did a little jig all the way to the door of the office. She grinned at Kathleen.

"Looks like you passed," Kathleen said.

"Yup!" Grace ran to the office door and threw it open. Eleven expectant faces gazed back at her. Her bunkmates had all come to wait for the results. *They are the best friends in the entire world,* she thought, touched.

"Well, don't keep us in suspense," Natalie said. "How did you do?"

"WetWorld, here we come!" Grace yelled.

"What's up, Gracie?" Gaby dropped down on the black box next to Grace at the start of drama class the next day.

Grace couldn't believe her ears. Gaby sounded completely friendly and normal. As if nothing had happened between them. As if they'd never had a disagreement in their lives.

"Did you see Tyler and Stephanie at breakfast this morning?" Gaby asked. "They were actually holding hands."

Grace shook her head. How could Gaby just pretend that things were okay between them? Did she expect Grace to forget her bad behavior? Still, Grace couldn't exactly be rude to her, not when Gaby was acting all nice like this.

"Um . . . I really have to cram," Grace said. "I didn't think my parents would let me audition, so I haven't even bothered to learn the scene." She turned back to her copy of *The Sound of Music*.

"No kidding," Gaby said. "I *am* your partner. I know we haven't been practicing." She sounded annoyed. But what did she have to be annoyed about?

Gaby still hadn't apologized for lying about her free-swim punishment, and here she was acting as if *Grace* was the difficult one.

"I'm sorry," Grace said, not entirely meaning it. "We could have been rehearsing an audition scene for you. You never mentioned it, so I just figured you weren't planning to try out for the play."

"It's more fun to have half an hour to play around during drama," Gaby said. "Who wants to spend time practicing?"

"Um, I do," Grace told her. "It's really important to me to get a part in the play this year." Gaby rolled her eyes, but Grace ignored her. "I'm going to do the scene from *The Sound of Music* like we talked about."

Gaby played around with the laces on her sneakers. She didn't seem to want to help, but Grace knew she had no choice. The first half hour of drama was for practicing. Bethany was cool about people sitting and talking quietly with their partners—she knew not everyone wanted to audition. But they weren't allowed to just goof around or wander away from their partners. So if she wanted to rehearse, Gaby was going to have to sit there and listen.

"It's the scene where she's teaching the kids to sing," Grace said, pulling the typed pages out of her notebook. She hadn't even looked at them since the second day of drama. She'd been too bummed about the fact that her folks wouldn't let her try out. But she had the movie *The Sound of Music* on DVD, so she knew the scene pretty well already. "You read the kids' lines. There aren't many." She handed over the pages.

Gaby heaved a huge sigh, as if Grace was asking her to climb a mountain or something.

By the time she'd said two lines, Gaby was yawning. And when it was Gaby's turn to speak, she was busy putting a little braid in her hair and missed her cue.

"You're supposed to be helping me," Grace said, frustrated. "You're the one who wanted to be partners."

"That's because I thought you would be fun," Gaby said. "I didn't know you actually wanted to try out for the stupid play."

Grace noticed Devon and Simon glancing over in her direction. "Shh," she told Gaby. "Other people are trying to rehearse."

"So?" Gaby's voice was as loud as ever.

"Why did you sign up for drama if you think the play is stupid?" Grace asked.

"Who said I signed up for it? I asked for photography, but Lizzie put me in drama."

"Why?" Grace asked.

Gaby shrugged. "My stupid bunkmate Christa is in photography, and Lizzie wanted to separate us."

"Because you stole her shampoo?" Grace said.

"I told you I didn't steal it," Gaby snapped. "Christa's just a crybaby."

Grace didn't answer. She had a feeling there was more to the story than Gaby was telling her. Based on her conversation with Julie and Marissa, Grace thought that Gaby had gotten in a lot of trouble for bullying Christa.

"Bethany, can I go to the restroom?" Gaby called out. When Bethany nodded, Gaby just got up and left without even glancing in Grace's direction. *So much for having a scene partner,* Grace thought, exasperated. *I can't believe I ever thought she could be my best friend.*

"Psst, Grace." Devon leaned toward her. "You can

practice with us if you want. We'll read lines for your scene and you can read lines for ours."

"Really?" Grace said.

Devon and Simon both nodded.

"Wow. Thanks." She grabbed her stuff and headed over to them. She tried not to look at Devon's friendly face. If she did, she knew she'd get tongue-tied and not even be able to read her scene. All she could do was hope that it would be easier talking to Devon using words that someone else had thought up!

▲ ▲ ▲

Dear Emily,

I'm sorry, I'm sorry, I'm sorry. (Repeat at least a hundred times.)

You were right. You said I would be too busy having fun to write to you this summer. And at first I was. But then I got too busy not having fun. There's this girl Gaby from bunk 3A—that's right, those evil girls I told you about last year. Anyway, most of those girls are actually okay. But this one is mean. Kind of. Sometimes. She started out being all nice to me, and she was funny. So I thought maybe she could be my camp best friend. Not that I'm trying to replace you!! But it stinks that you're not here. So I figured I could be friends with Gaby. And as soon as we were friends, she started being weird. Sometimes she's mean, but then she always says she's only joking. You know me—I have a good sense of humor. So why can't I tell when she's kidding around? I guess I just really missed having one best friend, a partner in crime. But you know what they say—with friends like that! I guess it just goes to show that you really are irreplaceable!

Anyway, I thought I would let you know that I finished The Call of the Wild. Mom and Dad made me take a quiz on it, and I got everything right. Now I just have to read The Jungle Book. I think it will be easy after this one. So, I kept my deal with them to read the book, and now I'm keeping my deal with you. I promised to write and I'm writing!

I wish you were here. You could tell me what to do about the situation with Gaby. I don't think I really want to be friends with her, but I also can't stand the thought of being mean or hurting her feelings. Maybe I'm too soft? Who knows. Cross your fingers that I figure it out soon.

See you in less than a month!

Grace

"Do, a deer, a female deer!" Grace sang as she swept the floor during chores on Wednesday. "Re, a drop of golden sun!"

"Meeee, a name I call myseeeelf!" Jenna screeched in a fake falsetto voice.

Everybody cracked up. Grace felt a little bad. They were all probably sick of hearing that song. "Sorry," she said.

"Grace, you've been practicing nonstop for two days," Alyssa said. "Take a break before you make yourself hoarse."

"Yeah, you'll make yourself hoarse," Candace added.

"Besides, you know the whole scene really well," Valerie said. She lowered her voice. "You learned it much faster than Brynn did." Brynn was outside, running lines with Alex as they walked to the Dumpster to throw out the garbage.

"Nah, she's just a perfectionist," Grace said. "Plus, Brynn's had more time to rehearse. Auditions are in an hour and I'm totally not ready."

"Yes, you are ready," Marissa said. "You were singing in your sleep last night."

"Seriously, Grace, you're a natural," Natalie said. "You'll definitely get a part. And then you'll be the huge celebrity at camp, and everyone will forget all about my father!"

Grace smiled nervously. "I'm finished sweeping. Is it okay if I go over to the drama shack to practice before auditions?"

"Go ahead," Julie said. "Break a leg!"

"Thanks." Grace pushed through the door and bounded down the steps. To her surprise, Karen was sitting on the grass in front of the porch. "Hey. Whatcha doing?" Grace asked.

Karen jumped. "Oh! I'm, um, I'm on dusting duty. I came out here to shake out the duster." She held up their ancient feather duster as evidence.

"You're shaking out the duster while sitting down?" Grace asked, confused.

"No." Karen got up quickly. "I was . . . uh . . ."

"Hiding from Chelsea?" Grace guessed.

Karen's gaze dropped to her sneakers. "No. Of course not."

"Karen, I heard you guys talking the other day," Grace said. "I know you're bummed about having to skip the rides at the water park."

"No, it's okay," Karen said. "Chelsea doesn't like rides."

"But you do," Grace pointed out.

"Yeah, but I don't want to leave Chelsea alone," Karen said. "That wouldn't be very nice. I already told her I'd hang out with her." She gave the duster a little shake. "I better finish my chores." She hurried up the steps but turned back before going in. "Hey, Grace, good luck at your audition," she said quietly. "I think you're the best actress at camp." Then she disappeared into the bunk.

Grace started down the trail. All her nervousness had returned the second Karen mentioned the tryout. It was nice to know that her bunkmates thought so highly of her, but she felt completely unprepared for the audition. She'd had to do all the work on her scene by herself. Gaby hadn't even bothered to check in and see how it was going.

But when she got to the drama shack for tryouts, Gaby was there, sitting in the "audience"—a bunch of the black boxes turned upside down for people to sit on while they watched the auditions. Grace was touched. Maybe Gaby hadn't been the best drama partner in the world, but at least she was there to support Grace when it mattered. It was the first best-friend-like thing Gaby had ever done. Only a real friend would realize how nervous Grace would be about the audition. If Emily had been at Camp Lakeview, she would've been there to show her support. And for once, Gaby was acting the same way. She was being supportive.

"Hey," Grace said, sitting on the box next to Gaby. "Thanks for coming."

"Why wouldn't I come?" Gaby said. "I think I have a pretty good shot at landing a part."

Grace couldn't believe her ears. "You're auditioning?" she asked.

"Of course."

"But you didn't even practice," Grace cried. "You said you thought the play was stupid!"

"It is," Gaby said. "That's why I didn't bother practicing. How hard can it be to get a role in *Peter Pan?* It's a kiddie story!"

Bethany clapped her hands for attention, so Grace couldn't answer. She wouldn't have known how to respond, anyway. Gaby hadn't come here to support Grace at all. Gaby was only here for herself!

Auditions went in age order, so the younger kids went first. Most of them forgot a line or two, but a few were very good singers. By the time it was the third division's turn, the butterflies in Grace's stomach felt more like a flock of birds. "Third division, who's first?" Bethany called.

"Me!" Brynn leapt up and ran to the front of the room. "I'm doing the scene from *The Music Man.*"

"I think I'll volunteer to go next," Grace whispered to Gaby. "I'm so nervous, I just want to get it over with."

Brynn did an amazing job on her tryout. Grace had heard her do the scene a hundred times over the past week, but seeing her perform it today was like watching it for the first time. Brynn disappeared and Marion the librarian stood onstage talking and singing. When she was done, Grace clapped and whistled through her teeth. "Way to go, Brynn!" she yelled.

"Thank you, Brynn," Bethany said. "Who's next?"

"I am!" Gaby called, jumping up and heading to the makeshift stage. Grace almost laughed. Gaby's behavior was so awful all the time that Grace wasn't even surprised anymore when she acted rudely. *It's my own fault for telling her I wanted to go next,* she thought. *I should've known that would make her steal my slot for herself.*

Gaby did the scene from *The Sound of Music.* She forgot half the lines and only sang one verse of the song. But she looked totally proud of herself when she was done. Grace clapped politely, and then raised her hand to go next.

As she passed by on her way up to the front of the room, Devon whispered "good luck," and Simon gave her a thumbs-up. Grace smiled back. They'd been much more helpful to her than her own partner had—they'd gone through the scene with her three times the other day.

Once she got on stage, Grace forgot all about Gaby and her obnoxious behavior. She forgot about *The Call of the Wild* and the quiz. She forgot about the fact that she still had to read *The Jungle Book* before camp ended. She even forgot about the water-park trip the next day. Her entire mind was focused on being Maria, the nun-turned-nanny, teaching the von Trapp kids to sing. She spoke the lines and sang the song as if the words were coming straight from her own brain, not as if she'd memorized them and practiced them over and over. The black room around her became the grassy hills of Austria, and the people watching became the children she was talking to.

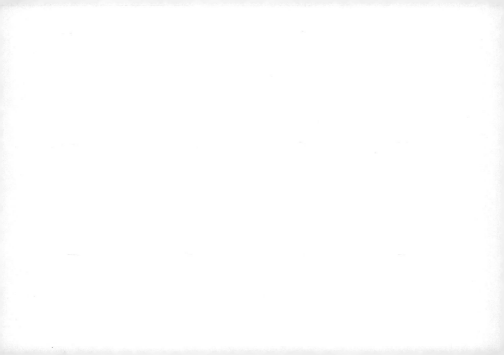

TALENT SHOW

Hiya, _____,
<u>NAME OF PERSON</u>

There were so many gifted singers and _____
<u>PLURAL NOUN</u>

in our talent _____, you would have
<u>NOUN</u>

thought it was an audition for _____
<u>ADJECTIVE</u>

Idol. My favorite was an eleven-year-old rap

_____, who had the audience in the palm of his
<u>NOUN</u>

_____. When he finished _____,
<u>PART OF THE BODY</u>   <u>VERB ENDING IN "ING"</u>

the _____ audience rose to their
<u>ADJECTIVE</u>

_____ and gave him a standing _____.
<u>PART OF THE BODY (PLURAL)</u>   <u>NOUN</u>

Believe me, he was a tough _____ to follow.
<u>NOUN</u>

I sang a medley of _____ from Broadway
<u>PLURAL NOUN</u>

_____. If I do say so myself, I was a/an
<u>PLURAL NOUN</u>

_____ hit. I received seven curtain _____.
<u>ADJECTIVE</u>   <u>PLURAL NOUN</u>

From your _____ Broadway star,
<u>ADJECTIVE</u>

_____
<u>YOUR NAME</u>

FROM: _____
_____
_____

TO: _____
_____
_____

MAD LIBS

INFIRMARY

Hey, _____,

NAME OF PERSON

Yesterday, I sprained my _____ and

PART OF THE BODY

scraped my _____ when I tripped on a

NOUN

tennis _____ during a/an _____ match

NOUN ADJECTIVE

against a friend. Don't worry, I was _____

ADVERB

sent to the infirmary. They have a/an _____

ADJECTIVE

doctor and a registered _____ on duty 24/7.

NOUN

The doctor asked me to roll up my _____ and

NOUN

then examined me _____. He said I'm okay and

ADVERB

left me in the capable _____ of the nurse. She

PLURAL NOUN

cleaned my _____ cut with antiseptic and

ADJECTIVE

_____ wrapped a bandage around my

ADVERB

_____. It took all of twenty minutes before

PART OF THE BODY

I was back hitting _____ on the tennis court.

PLURAL NOUN

Your sore _____,

NOUN

_____

YOUR NAME

From LETTERS FROM CAMP MAD LIBS • Copyright © 2006 by Price Stern Sloan.
Printed for promotional edition of CAMP CONFIDENTIAL, published by Grosset & Dunlap.
Price Stern Sloan and Grosset & Dunlap are divisions of Penguin Young Readers Group,
345 Hudson Street, New York, New York 10014.

FROM: _____
_____
_____

TO: _____
_____
_____

MAD☺LIBS

FIELD TRIP

Hi, _____,
NAME OF PERSON

Yesterday was a very _____ day. Early in the
ADJECTIVE

morning, we piled into a big yellow _____ and
NOUN

drove to Six _____ amusement park. The younger
PLURAL NOUN

kids spent the day riding the _____ on the
PLURAL NOUN

merry-go-round, playing video _____, and gobbling
PLURAL NOUN

up cotton _____. All of us older _____
PLURAL NOUN   PLURAL NOUN

headed for the roller _____. Wow, it's still a scary
NOUN

ride. I covered my _____–and that was on
PART OF THE BODY (PLURAL)

the way up. Coming down, we must have been going one

hundred _____ an hour. I swear my
PLURAL NOUN

_____ was in my mouth, and I just knew I was
PART OF THE BODY

going to _____ up. As suddenly as it began, the
VERB

_____ ride was over. I immediately got back in
ADJECTIVE

line to buy a/an _____ for the next ride.
NOUN

Your dizzy _____,
NOUN

_____
YOUR NAME

From LETTERS FROM CAMP MAD LIBS • Copyright © 2006 by Price Stern Sloan.
Printed for promotional edition of CAMP CONFIDENTIAL, published by Grosset & Dunlap.
Price Stern Sloan and Grosset & Dunlap are divisions of Penguin Young Readers Group.
345 Hudson Street, New York, New York 10014.

MAD LIBS

FROM: _____

_____

_____

TO: _____

_____

_____

MAD LIBS

She loved singing, and she knew the kids would, too. All she wanted in the world was to show these boys and girls how much joy there was in music, so she sang with every bit of happiness she had ever felt in her life.

When her song ended, Grace slowly became aware that people were clapping. She had to shake her head a little to clear away the image of the outdoors and the von Trapp kids. She'd been so wrapped up in her acting that she'd forgotten where she really was.

Breathing hard from singing, she took a bow and headed back out into the audience. Gaby sat with a sour expression on her face, barely clapping. Brynn was practically bouncing up and down on her black box, making whooping sounds as she applauded. Devon and Simon sat nearby, clapping and cheering, too. Grace didn't even hesitate.

She walked right by Gaby and sat with her other friends.

▲ ▲ ▲

"And Devon was amazing, too," Brynn said at dessert that night. "If only we were really doing *The Sound of Music*, he'd be an excellent Captain von Trapp."

"Then you two could act together, Grace," Natalie teased her.

"Don't you want to hear how your boyfriend, Simon, did?" Grace teased back. "I'm surprised you didn't sneak out of arts and crafts to come watch him audition."

"I thought about it," Natalie replied. "But instead I made him a little plate in pottery that says 'Congratulations.' I can't give it to him until he finds out if he got a part, though!"

Grace shook her head. It was no fun to tease Natalie about Simon these days. She just never got ruffled about it anymore. Not that she'd ever really been bothered by the teasing—if she had, Grace wouldn't have done it.

"I think he'll get a part," Brynn said. "He did a good job. I think we'll all get parts."

"Yeah, we rule," Grace agreed. "Are you still hoping for Wendy, Brynn? A lot of those division four and division five girls were really good." Brynn had done an incredible audition, but Grace didn't want her to get her hopes up too high. Despite what Bethany said, everybody knew that the main roles always went to older kids.

"They were good, but I still think I have a chance," Brynn said confidently. "And so do you."

"Okay, enough drama talk," Julie interrupted from her seat at the end of the bunk's table. "I know you two are dying to go look at the cast list."

"Bethany said she was going to post it after dinner," Brynn replied. "It's not up yet."

"Well . . ." Julie grinned. "I happen to know that she put it up on her way over to the mess hall. She just figured no one would know it was there until after dinner."

Brynn leapt up from her seat. "Can we go now?" she asked excitedly. "Please please please?"

"Go ahead," Julie said. "Good luck!"

Brynn grabbed Grace's hand and pulled her toward the door. By the time they got to the drama shack, everyone at Lakeview seemed to know that the list had been posted. A crowd of kids stood around the bulletin board on the outside of the shack.

"How are we supposed to see if we're on the list when we can't even see the list?" Grace joked.

"That's a total upset!" one of the division four kids said.

"I can't believe it," another older girl murmured. "I've been coming here for years, and no one that young has ever gotten such a big part."

"Maybe it's one of us!" Brynn cried happily.

Grace stood on her tiptoes, but she still couldn't see the list. "What are you guys talking about?" she asked the older girl.

"A third division girl got the part of Wendy," the girl said. "It's unheard of."

"Oh, it's not such a big deal," Brynn said modestly. "I've been studying acting since I was really little, so it's no surprise."

"Well, you'll probably be surprised to hear it's not you," Gaby said, pushing her way out of the crowd around the list.

Brynn's face fell. "What do you mean? They said it was someone from division three."

"Yeah," Gaby said. "That still doesn't mean it's you!"

"Why do you have to be so mean, Gaby?" Grace asked, putting her arm around Brynn's shoulders. "Brynn is really upset."

Suddenly Brynn gasped. "I am not upset!" she cried.

Grace glanced at her in surprise. "Why not?"

"Because I may not have gotten the part," she said, "but that can only mean one thing. *You* got it, Grace!"

chapter

ELEVEN

Grace woke up with a smile already on her face. It stayed there while she brushed her teeth and packed her backpack for the trip to WetWorld. It stayed there all through breakfast. And it was still in place when she climbed into the field-trip bus and started down the aisle.

She was playing Wendy in *Peter Pan!* And she was allowed to go to the water park! Just a week ago neither of those things had seemed possible.

Natalie and Alyssa had already grabbed one of the back seats, but there were lots of other campers in the little aisle between them and Grace. Ronald from 3E had a backpack as big as his whole body, and he was trying to throw it up onto the overhead luggage rack. Traffic in the aisle stopped as he lifted it again and again, never getting it high enough.

"Do you want some help?" Jenna's brother Adam asked.

Ronald was a twerp, but he had a surprisingly loud voice. "Not from you," he snapped.

Grace sighed. The rivalry between bunk 3E and Adam's bunk, 3F, was just as strong as the one between her bunk and Gaby's. There was no way Ronald would ever take help from Adam or his friends. She leaned against the back of one of the seats and waited for the path to clear.

"Gracie, back here! I got us a seat," Gaby called. Grace twisted around to see Gaby in the very front seat, right behind the driver. She was waving and grinning as if they were the best of friends. Ever since the announcement that Grace had gotten the part, Gaby had been super friendly and supportive. That was nice enough, but Grace couldn't forget how nasty she'd been so many times before that.

"Um, I'm sitting with Alyssa and Natalie," she called back. "Remember?"

Gaby's face fell. "I thought you changed your mind about that," she said. "I apologized for telling them about your book. Don't you remember?"

Grace did remember. And she also remembered Gaby lying to her about being punished, tricking her into not swimming in the deep end, refusing to help her practice for the audition, and just generally being a bully. She did *not* remember ever changing her mind about sitting with Gaby on the field-trip bus.

But Gaby really did look upset. She was glancing frantically around at the other kids on the bus, and Grace suddenly realized that Gaby had no one else to sit with. Grace thought about it. Gaby didn't seem very popular with her own bunkmates. Whatever had happened between her and Christa must have made them all uncomfortable. And outside of Grace, Gaby didn't seem to have any other friends. Grace sighed. What did she have to lose? She was in such a good mood just being there and knowing about her role in the play. She doubted even Gaby could ruin her happiness today.

She stood on her tiptoes and waved to Nat and Alyssa, pointing back toward Gaby so they'd know where she was going. Alyssa waved back, but Natalie made an "are you crazy" face. Grace just shrugged.

"Excuse me," she said, turning to go back toward the front of the bus.

"You're going the wrong way!" somebody complained.

"You can't get through," another voice whined.

Why did she have to sit all the way in the front? Grace wondered. Gaby was only three seats away from her, but the aisle was stuffed with campers. "Okay, clear the way!" Grace yelled. She jumped up onto the seat next to her and began climbing over the back of the one in front of it.

"Good idea," Devon said.

Grace almost fell on her face. She hadn't realized he was standing so close, only five or six people behind her. And here she was climbing over seats like a . . . well, not like a *girl*. Chelsea would never do something that was so *not* graceful. Natalie probably wouldn't, either. Grace flushed. She was stuck with her left foot on one seat and her right foot on another. There was no choice. She kept climbing, her face on fire. Finally she reached Gaby's seat and plopped down.

"Well, *that* was stupid-looking," Gaby commented.

Grace's mouth fell open. She'd practically done acrobatics in front of Devon and the whole third division just so she could get back here to sit with Gaby, and that was the thanks she got.

"I can do it again," Grace said. "All the way back to Alyssa and Natalie's seat."

"No," Gaby said quickly. "I was only kidding."

Grace didn't answer. Gaby seemed to use that excuse whenever she did or said something mean. By this point, Grace knew that Gaby wasn't really kidding most of the time.

"What ride do you want to go on first?" Gaby asked.

Grace simply shrugged. It was going to be a long day.

"This line is too long," Gaby complained at the Flume of Fear.

"You've said that about every single ride so far," Grace pointed out.

"Let's go on Rio Rafting," Gaby said. She stepped out of line and started walking away. Grace didn't follow her. She was sick of Gaby's attitude—that she got to decide everything and that she assumed Grace would just go along with her. They'd gotten off the lines for the past two rides because Gaby didn't want to wait. In almost three hours at the water park, they'd managed to go on only one actual ride!

This time Grace was going to stay put. If Gaby wanted to leave, fine. Grace would go on the Flume of Fear alone, and then she'd go find her bunkmates. They were probably having a great time. And she'd blown them off in order to hang out with Gaby, whom she didn't even like.

Grace gasped as she realized it. All this time, she'd been annoyed at Gaby, or confused by her behavior, or sometimes even a little afraid of what Gaby would do next. But she'd never stopped to think about her own feelings about their friendship. But all of a sudden it seemed so clear. She didn't want to be friends with Gaby. Gaby was a jerk!

"Come *on*, Gracie," Gaby said loudly, stomping back over to the line. "I don't want to wait for this stupid ride."

"Well, I do," Grace said. "And stop calling me Gracie."

Gaby blinked in surprise. "Why?"

"Because I hate it. In third grade I got caught daydreaming one time and everyone called me Spacey Gracie for the rest of the year."

Gaby laughed.

"You would think that was funny," Grace mumbled.

"It is funny. You need to lighten up." Gaby grabbed her hand. "Come on, let's go on the rafts."

Grace pulled her hand away. "No," she said. "We'll just end up waiting on line there until you get bored, and then you'll leave again, and we'll lose our place in *another* line."

Gaby opened her mouth, then closed it again. She obviously had no idea how to deal with someone saying no to her. Grace wondered if it had ever happened before. Maybe her bunkmates had stood up to her, and that's why she wasn't friends with any of them. "Oh, fine," Gaby finally said. Then she stood there and sulked for the next ten minutes as the line crept forward. She sulked as they got onto the flume ride, and she sulked all the way through its dips and bumps and its one huge drop.

Grace was impressed. She thought it must be hard to sulk when you wanted to scream and wave your arms around like everyone else on the ride. But Gaby stuck to it.

"Okay, now let's go on Rio Rafting," Grace said as they walked out of the flume exit.

"Finally," Gaby exploded. She took off toward the

rafts. By the time Grace caught up with her, Gaby was already frowning again. "This line's too long," she said. "If you hadn't made me go on that stupid flume, we could've been at the front already."

"Gaby, it's a water park in the middle of the summer," Grace said. "All the rides are going to have lines. You have to deal with it."

"No I don't," Gaby replied. "Look, there's Christa near the front. Let's go cut her."

"We can't cut her," Grace cried, trying to ignore the dirty looks that the people in line were giving them.

"Sure we can. She'll let us." Gaby strode off toward the front of the line. Mortified, Grace followed her.

"Gaby," she murmured, catching up. "We could get thrown out of the park for cutting in line."

Gaby rolled her eyes. "Whatever. We'll just say Christa was holding our place."

They reached Gaby's bunkmate. Grace couldn't help noticing that Christa did not look happy to see them. Her big brown eyes filled with nervousness at the sight of Gaby.

"We're gonna go on with you," Gaby announced.

"No, I'm . . . um, I'm with Jill," Christa said in a voice so low that it was practically a whisper.

"I don't see her," Gaby said.

"She's in the bathroom."

"Her loss," Gaby said, stepping in front of Christa.

"Gaby, we're going to get in trouble." Christa's voice shook as if she might cry. The people behind her were glaring at all three of them.

"Oh, don't be such a baby," Gaby said. "We'll only get in trouble if you tell. And you won't, right? You already snitched on me once. If you do it again, you'll be worse than a snitch. You'll be a rat."

"Okay, okay." Christa stepped aside to make room for them. She shot Grace a panicked look. *She thinks I'm going to bully her, too,* Grace realized. The thought made her want to laugh. Here was Christa thinking she was a bully when in reality she was just Gaby's latest victim. Obviously Gaby had been pushing Christa around all summer, and for the past two weeks Grace had been letting Gaby push *her* around, too.

She didn't get it. She wasn't a shy, self-conscious person like Christa. Or even like Karen, who got bullied by Chelsea a lot. So why was she allowing Gaby to walk all over her?

"You know what?" she said. "I'm not going to do this."

"Do what?" Gaby asked.

"Cut in line," Grace said. "And I don't care if you call me a baby or make fun of me or whatever you're going to do."

"What are you talking about?" Gaby tried to sound innocent, but it didn't work.

"You know what I'm talking about," Grace said. "You're a bully, Gaby. It's not cool."

"Well, you're a loser who can't even read," Gaby shot back. But she didn't sound mean anymore. In fact, Grace thought she sounded frightened. She clearly didn't like it when someone stood up to her.

"I am not a loser," Grace told her. "I just didn't pay enough attention to my schoolwork last year because I was busy having fun. With my *real* best friend, who never tries to push me around like you do."

"Why don't you just leave us alone?" Gaby snapped.

"I should've known better than to hang out with a girl from 3C." She turned her back on Grace, pulling Christa along with her.

"You shouldn't let her cut you, Christa," Grace said. "She's going to keep bullying you until you say no."

But Christa didn't even have the guts to look back at Grace. *Oh, well,* Grace thought. *Maybe I set a good example for her to follow once she gets up her nerve.*

One of the women in line behind them gave Grace a thumbs-up.

"Thanks," Grace said. She walked away from the Rio Rafting line feeling better than she had since she'd gotten on the bus that morning. She hadn't wanted to be rude to Gaby, but telling her off felt great. Now all she wanted to do was to find her bunkmates and start having fun on this field trip.

She went straight to the wave pool. Chelsea and Karen were lying out on two of the lounge chairs next to the pool. Both of them were completely dry, and Chelsea's hair was perfect, as usual.

"Hey, you guys," Grace greeted them. "You haven't gone on a single water ride all day, have you?"

"No way," Chelsea said.

"It's a water park, you know," Grace teased her.

Chelsea shrugged. "I don't want chlorine in my hair."

"Suit yourself," Grace said. "Do you know where everyone else is?"

"I think they all went to the three-story-high waterslide to cheer Jenna on," Karen said. "No one else was brave enough to go on it."

"I'll do it if you will, Karen," Grace said.

Karen gazed back at her, eyes wide. Chelsea

frowned. "Karen's hanging out with me," she said. "I don't want to stay here all alone."

"Then you should come with us," Grace told her. "Come on, Karen. What do you say?"

Karen glanced at Chelsea. Then at Grace. "Well . . ." She took a deep breath. "Okay." She leapt up off her lounge chair and started walking away as fast as she could. *She's afraid Chelsea will stop her*, Grace thought. *And she's probably right.*

"Hey!" Chelsea cried.

Grace shrugged. "Sorry. You can come with us if you want."

For a split second, Chelsea looked as if she might. Then she shook her head. "No, thanks." She sat back in her chair and closed her eyes.

"Come find us if you get lonely," Grace said. Then she took off after Karen.

▲ ▲ ▲

"I can't believe you got us all on that waterslide," Natalie said half an hour later. "That was the most terrifying thing I've ever done in my whole life."

"I can't believe all you guys were willing to go on it just because Grace wanted you to," Jenna said. "You didn't even *think* of going on it to keep me company."

"You didn't need company," Alyssa pointed out. "You were brave enough to do it alone."

"Yeah, Jenna, I think I would have wimped out if you guys weren't with me," Karen said.

Grace grinned. Hanging out with her bunkmates was cool, but getting Karen to come out of her shell a little bit was even cooler. As soon as Grace had announced that

Karen wanted to go on the slide, all the other girls had agreed to join in. Everybody knew that Chelsea bullied Karen, but no one had ever had the nerve to say anything about it before. Now that Karen had taken a stand, they all wanted to support her. Grace could tell how much the support meant to Karen.

It's how I felt when they all helped me study for Mom's quiz, she thought. *Like I was surrounded by the best group of friends in the world.*

"Who wants to play Shoot-the-Starfish?" Alex asked.

"Not me," Sarah replied. "But I am a little shaky after that thirty-foot drop. I'll go play one of the other games."

"Yeah, I want to keep my feet on the ground for a few minutes," Valerie agreed. "That slide was fun, but it knocked me out!"

"So let's go over to the arcade, and we'll all play whatever games we want for half an hour," Grace suggested. "Then we can do the Tarzan rope-swing ride."

When they got to the arcade, Brynn took off for the karaoke booth. Alex and Jenna headed to Shoot-the-Starfish. Karen went with Sarah and Valerie to check out the ancient video games like Pac-Man.

"Let's play that Loch Ness game," Natalie said.

Grace glanced over to the game, which was basically Whack-a-Mole with miniature Loch Ness monsters instead of moles. The game looked pretty boring. But playing the game at that moment were Simon, Adam, and Devon.

"Yeah. Let's go," Alyssa said, trying to sound casual.

Grace burst out laughing. "You guys are so obvious!" she said. "You just want to hang out with your boyfriends."

"Adam is not my boyfriend," Alyssa said.

"But you want him to be," Nat replied.

"Not as much as you want Simon to be yours," Alyssa shot back.

"Please," Grace said. "You both like them, and they like you. It's disgusting."

"Well, you like Devon," Nat said.

"I do not."

"Fine," Alyssa put in. "Then let's not go play the Loch Ness game." She exchanged a smile with Natalie, and they both stared at Grace, waiting for her reaction.

Grace thought about it. Devon *was* cute. And he was a good actor. And he seemed to like her. He'd helped her prepare for auditions, and he'd complimented her a few times now. But that didn't mean she *liked* him. Still . . . it couldn't hurt to play the same arcade game he was playing. And her friends really wanted to hang out with his friends. "No, that's okay," she said aloud. "We can play the Loch Ness game. It looks like fun."

She led the way over to the game booth, ignoring the fact that Natalie and Alyssa were totally laughing at her.

By the time they got to the booth, the boys were at the front, each armed with a giant rubber-tipped mallet. A buzzer rang, and the little Nessie heads began popping up from holes in the board along the front of the booth. Immediately the guys went to work, smashing the mallets down on anything they could hit.

Natalie and Alyssa cheered loudly, and Grace couldn't help but join in. When the buzzer rang again to signal the end of the game, Adam had one Nessie hit and Simon had two. Neither one of them qualified to win anything. But Devon had five hits.

"Choose your prize," said the guy in the Scottish hat behind the counter. "A stuffed Nessie or a stuffed lobster."

Devon turned around. "Grace, which one do you want?" he asked.

Grace told herself to ignore the fact that Nat's eyes were bugging out of her head and Alyssa's gasp was so loud that everyone in the park could hear it. It was harder, though, to ignore the heat creeping up her neck, signaling that she was about to turn bright red from embarrassment.

"Um, the Nessie," she said.

The Scottish-hat guy handed over a little stuffed animal that looked like a brontosaurus wearing a plaid scarf. And Devon turned and gave it to Grace.

Don't be a dork this time, she ordered herself. *Come up with something cool to say.*

"Thanks," she said.

Devon just nodded, flashing one of his adorable smiles.

"Now when people say the Loch Ness monster is just a legend, I can show them this to prove it really exists," Grace added. There! That was at least a little bit of her true personality.

Devon laughed. "Yeah, it would be hard to argue with that."

"Let's go play the water-ski game," Adam said. "I'm better at that one." The boys took off toward the interactive games. Devon hesitated for a moment. "Did you know I got a role as one of the Lost Boys?" he asked.

136

"Yeah, congratulations," Grace said. "I knew you'd get a part. Your audition was amazing."

"Not as amazing as yours. You have real talent," he said seriously. "But now that we're both in the play, maybe we can run lines together to practice."

Grace felt a strange little tingle move up the back of her neck. "Sure. That would be fun."

"Cool." Devon gave her a little wave as he walked off after his friends. Grace realized that she was still grinning stupidly, but somehow she couldn't make herself stop.

"You were right about that Loch Ness game, Grace," Alyssa said as Natalie collapsed into a fit of giggles. "It *was* fun."

"Fun to watch you flirt with Devon!" Natalie crowed.

"Just because Devon and I are friends doesn't mean I like him," Grace said.

"Yeah, right," Natalie replied.

"It doesn't," Grace insisted. "We're just going to practice for the play together. That's all."

They both smirked at her, and she couldn't blame them. As much as she hated to admit it, she kind of had a crush on Devon. "Okay, we believe you," Alyssa told her, obviously lying.

"Good," Grace said. "Because I don't like boys. It is a cute Nessie, though."

▲ ▲ ▲

"You guys had Grace for the whole time at the arcade," Valerie said. She grabbed Grace's arm as soon as they all got out into the parking lot where the bus was. "Sarah and I get her for the ride home."

Natalie pouted. "She was supposed to sit with us on the way there and she didn't. I think we should get her now."

"Ladies, ladies, there's enough of me to go around," Grace joked. "Let's just sit right across from one another. That way we all can still talk."

"We'll sit in front of you," Jenna added, following them. "Our whole bunk should sit together."

"Yeah, then Grace and I can practice our scenes for you on the way," Brynn suggested. She was playing a Lost Boy in the play, and Grace was grateful that Brynn didn't seem to be mad at her for getting a bigger part.

With everyone laughing and talking—except Chelsea, who was grumpy because she'd gotten a sunburn—they made their way to the big field-trip bus. Just as Grace was about to climb the tall steps, Gaby walked up next to her and gave her a little shove to push her out of the way.

"Hey!" Grace yelped. "You almost knocked me over!"

"Oh, sorry." Gaby sneered at her. "I guess I'm not supposed to touch you now that you're such a big star."

"You're not supposed to push anyone out of the way whether they're a big star or not," Brynn snapped, stepping up to defend Grace.

"What do you care?" Gaby said. "She stole the part you wanted!"

"She won the part fair and square," Brynn said. "That's part of being an actor, so I have to learn to deal with it. I'm not going to hold a grudge against my friend for doing a better audition than me."

"You wouldn't understand that, though," Alex

said, coming to Brynn's side. "You obviously don't know anything about being a true friend."

"Yeah, you don't know anything about it," Candace put in.

"You're just a bully," Chelsea said. "Everybody knows it."

A few of the girls in 3C exchanged smiles. That was the pot calling the kettle black! But it was nice to have everyone in 3C standing together. They really did work well as a team.

"You're all losers, anyway," Gaby said. "I don't know what I was thinking making friends with someone from your lame bunk." She scurried into the bus to get away from them.

"Say what you want, it won't bother us," Jenna called after her. "We know how cool we are."

"So cool that we have the two best actresses in the third division," Alyssa said.

"And Jenna and Alex, the best athletes," Natalie added.

"And we're the scavenger-hunt champs," Sarah said.

"And we're totally going to win color war," Valerie put in.

By now, they were all laughing. "Plus, we're the smartest, prettiest girls in the entire known universe," Grace joked. "And we're extremely modest."

Grace felt a swell of happiness as her bunkmates all high-fived one another. Why had she thought she needed a friend outside of the bunk? They all climbed into the bus and made their way toward the back seats.

Grace noticed Gaby sitting with Christa near the front. Gaby pointedly looked away when Grace passed.

Oh, well, Grace thought. *I guess that's the end of our friendship.* She had lots of problems with Gaby's behavior, but Grace had a hard time staying mad at people. She'd hoped that they could at least be friendly to each other, even if they weren't going to be best friends. But Gaby clearly didn't see it that way.

"Come on, Grace!" Sarah called. "We saved the aisle seat for you."

Grace hurried back to the group of seats her friends had taken over. "It's bunk 3C on wheels," she said. Everyone laughed as she plopped into her seat, letting her stress over Gaby melt away.

Who needed *one* best friend when you had eleven?

Turn the page for a sneak preview of

camp
CONFIDENTIAL

Alex's Challenge

available now!

chapter
ONE

Jenna was addicted to sugar. Sometimes, she had cupcakes. Other times, she passed out Swedish fish. That night, she had the largest quantity of Nerds that Alex had ever seen. The round, little balls of candy were pink and purple. As Jenna passed them around—you had to admit she was awfully generous—some Nerds inevitably went flying. Gnat-sized streaks of unnatural color dashed through the air like Fourth of July sparklers. Alex couldn't help it; she peeked up to watch the scene, her mouth beginning to water. She loved the sharp, sweet flavor of Nerds in particular. Just as she was going back to writing her letter, a handful of the hard sugar pellets nicked her left cheek.

"Agh!" Alex yelled. Those buggers really hurt.

Some girls started to grumble while others laughed. After six weeks together, everyone knew the grumblers (Chelsea, Karen, and Alyssa) from the goofballs (Jenna, Grace, and Natalie) without even giving it much thought. That's what had happened at Camp Lakeview every year Alex had been there: The girls would get "thisclose," and sometimes there was this magical warm and fuzzy feeling between them, like you'd met eleven soul mates. Other times, like during the War of the Nerds, "thisclose" was a catalyst for crankiness.

"Hey, did you get some?" Valerie asked Alex quietly.

"Yeah, they left bruises on my cheek," Alex answered as usual. "Seriously, though, I don't want any," she added. This time, Alex went back to writing her letter for real. She had to concentrate on seeming busy; that way the girls were less likely to pay attention to her. Alex wouldn't disturb a fly—and she liked herself that way. She was the original get-along girl and never caused commotion. She didn't even yell at Jenna's twin brother, Adam, when he snapped her bra strap earlier that day. Except for Brynn, who was her best camp friend, most people didn't know what made her tick. Maybe Brynn didn't even know.

"Okay, cool," Val said. "More for me then."

"I *know* you didn't just hit me in the eye!" Chelsea yelled into the air. Lights-out was in fifteen minutes, but she was always in bed first. She claimed that her face broke out if she didn't get enough beauty sleep. Chelsea even tried to get the other girls to quiet down early, as if that would've ever worked.

"Aye, aye, Captain Chelsea," Grace mimicked. "You better watch out, or you might lose a tongue, too."

"Grace, please stop," Chelsea said.

"Oh, we're just having fun," Jenna said. With so many brothers and sisters, she was pretty good at keeping the peace—as long as she wasn't at war with Adam.

"Well, not to be a party pooper . . ." said Natalie. She was the daughter of the hot movie star Tad Maxwell. Alex had to hand it to Natalie; Natalie wasn't stuck-up

143

or glamorous or Hollywood at all. (She did love teen magazines, but that was forgivable.) "But I have to sweep the floor tomorrow, and you all are making things more difficult," Natalie continued.

"Boo!" said Alyssa, Natalie's best friend. Alyssa, a funky, artsy girl, hurled a few more candies at Chelsea just for fun.

"I *said* stop it!" Chelsea yelled again. Karen went over to calm Chelsea down, and it was clear they were gossiping about everyone else. Brynn and Grace started talking about the *Peter Pan* play again, and other girls rolled their eyes. Natalie and Alyssa whispered something to each other, and so did Valerie and Sarah.

Alex just didn't get it. They were all down about something. Natalie was worried about Simon, who hadn't come to talk to her during free period that day. Grace complained about her parents, who were making her read *The Jungle Book*. Chelsea whined that she needed a nose job (she so didn't—her beak was as cute as a Barbie doll's). Jenna said that Adam was driving her insane because he kept asking about her bunkmates without telling her which one he was interested in. Brynn didn't know how on earth she'd memorize all of her lines in time to perfect the voice she would need in order to deliver them.

Alex breathed in deeply, trying not to get teary-eyed. She knew it wasn't nice of her to be jealous of them, but she was. She would've traded any one of their problems—she would even take two or three of their issues at once!—to get rid of her own. She wanted to know what it was like to be stress-free. She would've given her athletic ability—all of it—for just one day where she didn't have to worry, worry, and worry some more. There she was with the girls who knew her best, if anyone knew her at all, and still, Alex felt totally alone.

Chelsea, surprisingly, had risen from bed and walked over to Jenna's bottom bunk in her pink-feathered night slippers. Who knew what she said to Jenna, but she went back to her bed with a new handful of Nerds.

"You want some, Alex?" Chelsea asked, interrupting Alex who was deep in thought. She hadn't been concentrating on the letter, but she was a pro when it came to making it look like she was.

Alex tried to be as casual and busy as she could when she answered, "No, thank you." She started writing on her sheet of paper energetically. She wanted it to look like she was inspired so no one would want to break her train of deep thought. No one would've wanted to, either—no one except Chelsea.

"What? Are you watching your weight?" Chelsea said, grabbing the satin sleep mask she wore at night.

"No," Alex said sharply, fighting that teary-eyed feeling as hard as she could.

"Hey, everyone, maybe we should try to be as slim and trim and perfect as Alex," Chelsea remarked.

Alex held a death grip on her pen. She poked a hole through her paper with it. She wanted to scream, to rip Chelsea's pink slippers to shreds. But mostly, she just hoped that no one could tell how flustered she was at that moment.

"No," Alex said. She had been born with a naturally slender, stereotypically Korean body like her mother's. The truth was, Alex couldn't gain weight if she ate every single box of Nerds produced at the Nerd factory. Tired of always being the skinny girl, she had tried everything she could to pack on some pounds. She ate super-sized combo meals, protein shakes, and cheese-oozing Italian foods—her body stayed as tight and fat-free as a hardback book. So a year ago, Alex started working out to build muscles and bulk up that way. To her surprise, she found out she was really good at sports—all sports—but especially soccer and swimming. Being athletic that summer had started building her confidence. Being teased for her pickiness was breaking her down.

"Lights out!" Julie, their counselor, yelled. Alex was thankful to be rescued.

Valerie got out of bed lightning fast to flick off the night lamps. The girls went back to whispering about whatever as Alex cried herself to sleep.

▲ ▲ ▲

"Final electives!" Julie yelled the next morning. Everyone needed to pick their final free-choice classes for the last two weeks at Camp Lakeview.

Alex huddled with her best friend, Brynn, to make the big decision. Brynn was such a drama queen, and Alex couldn't have been more opposite. For that reason, their friendship worked. Brynn created action and excitement. Alex loved her for it—Brynn kept Alex from ever getting bored.

"I have to take drama, of course," Brynn said.

"Is there any chance I could talk you into taking ceramics with me? Pleeeease!" Alex whined. She wished she and her best friend could finally have a class together. After all, there was no way Alex could take drama—she considered herself allergic to the spotlight.

"Just take drama with me," Brynn said. "I'll help you! It

would be so cool. You never know—you might be a star."

"No," Alex answered. "No, no, and no."

"I love you, Alex, but you can't ask me to give up my whole entire life for you," Brynn said, kind of teasing, kind of not teasing.

"Okay, okay," Alex relented.

The other girls from the best bunk, 3C of course, flocked to Julie's sign-up clipboard. Julie was always smiling, and everyone loved her. It didn't even bother her to get bum-rushed. While Alex waited patiently for the mob to clear, she heard Jenna sign up for photography again with her brother Adam. Alex was happy to see they were getting along better again. Jenna'd had a rough spot a few weeks ago when she'd pulled a crazy prank, letting all of the animals free to howl and poop and cry during the camp social. Grace and Brynn signed up for drama and vowed to be partners. Natalie and Alyssa asked to be on the newspaper together, and Val, always the free spirit, signed up for woodworking.

"You just want to be with the boys!" Chelsea teased her.

"I'm not stupid," she said, flipping her long cornrows into Chelsea's face. Alex knew that Val was just playing along, though. Val was really good at woodworking whether more boys happened to be in that class or not. She'd already made a cutting board, a lamp, and a carved plaque with an elephant on it that she'd hung on her bunk.

When the coast was clear, Alex made her move.

"Here comes young Mia Hamm," Julie said, making Alex blush. "So, what'll it be?"

"Ceramics, please," she answered. Alex had seen the

necklaces some girls had made in the last session. They were these shiny, round beads that hung from a leather strap. Alex knew her mother, an art teacher, would love to have one. She was so excited to be in ceramics that she had saved that class for last.

"Wait, um, Alex," Julie called a few seconds later. "Could you please do me a favor?"

"Sure, anything," Alex said. Julie was truly cool. Anyone would do anything for her.

"I see that ceramics is full, and I promised Christa from 3B that she could be in the class because of all the trouble she's been having with Gaby," Julie said.

"Um, well," Alex said, feeling her hopes sink into the hungry part of her stomach. "Okay," she added. Alex didn't know how to say no even though she desperately wanted to. She visualized kicking herself for not signing up for ceramics earlier. *It's my own fault*, she thought.

"Sweetie, you are *the best*," Julie said, hugging her. "I know I can always count on my awesome Mia Hamm."

Alex smiled widely. She loved making other people happy, especially Julie. She watched as Julie found Christa, a shy girl with few friends, and told her she would be in ceramics. Christa's eyes and smile were gigantic. Alex was disappointed, but she felt so good about giving up her spot. She had done the right thing; she was sure of it. But then why, at that moment, did she feel so sad?

chapter

TWO

When Alex was on the soccer field, there was no Chelsea to antagonize her. There were no free-choice mishaps. There was no Brynn overdramatizing about her drama class. There were no cranky campmates. There was, for once, only Alex. And she was the star.

She had been looking forward to the afternoon because that day, for their usual post-breakfast bunk activity, her mates were taking on their rivals, the girls from 3A. Both bunks had chosen to play soccer. When the announcement was made, Alex felt like she would finally have a good day, and she was right. As usual, she had been chosen as the leader of her 3C team, and that made her feel confident. She wasn't the fastest runner—Sarah had that strength. She also wasn't the strongest goalie—Jenna could make that claim. But Alex *was* the most fearless player. The ball was her pet. Alex could skillfully follow it, volley it, chase it, and kick it as if it were attached to her Diadora soccer cleats. The soccer ball met its match every time Alex took to the field.

But the other team, the girls from bunk 3A, was playing a really good game. Alex wanted to win, and the score was six for her team, eight for the enemies, er, opponents. She started to freak out. Alex would rather lick bugs every day for two weeks than lose a game of soccer. She thought of her favorite childhood book, *The Little Engine That Could*. She knew it was silly, but that story—one her mother had read to her once a week from nursery school through the first grade—always got her spirits up. She'd tell herself, "I think I can, I think I can," whenever she got nervous before a test or game or meeting with a teacher. Then during whatever made her nervous, she'd change the words to: "I know I can, I know I can."

Today, with the other team's score creeping up, she added another line to the cheerleader in her head. She thought, *I know I can. I know we can. I know, I know, I know.* She didn't like to brag or anything—bragging was bad manners according to Alex—but she had to get herself psyched to win three more points and take the game. As the next time-out happened, she took charge—something she'd been doing a lot this summer—and gave the only advice she knew that would help them win.

"You all are awesome! You are better than these girls! You can kick their tails—I've seen you do it before. Now come on!" she yelled. The girls from 3C just watched her.

Candace said, "We can kick their tails!"

Jessie yelled, "You betcha!"

Others stood in the huddle with their mouths open. Some were really passionate about soccer, but most just saw it as a way to have some fun. Those who weren't as competitive were the ones Alex had to get pumped up.

"My shins are getting sore," Alyssa said, bending over to rub them.

"My throat hurts," Chelsea whined, twirling her

hair around her pointer finger.

That's when Valerie stepped in, "You all are fine. You have to be! We're gonna win!" Valerie was always like that—she had the sunniest attitude of anybody. Alex was starting to realize that Val was never, ever in a bad mood.

"That's right, we are," Jenna added with pursed lips and furrowed brows. She took soccer as seriously as Alex did.

"Who's the best?!" Alex yelled, relieved that the whiners—there were always two or three on every team—had been shut down. She was even more relieved that Valerie had been the one to do it. She was such a cool girl. No one could argue with Valerie.

"Um, you are," Natalie answered, looking at Alex.

"No!" Alex laughed. "*We* are!"

After the pep talk, Alex started talking strategy. She told Sarah to run past the other team's best runner—that would distract her from the game at hand. Jenna had three girls to cover. Brynn was supposed to stand near the goal and block anyone who came toward Alex when she went in for the point. Even the whiners came on board for the winning plans. By the end of the time-out, no one was unmotivated anymore. Instead, their expressions were determined. The girls looked like they took this game seriously, and even better, they looked like they wanted to win.

They huddled up in a circle like a bunch of NFL football stars and yelled their bunk cheer, "We be 3C!" It wasn't poetry, but it was catchy. They high-fived and cheered one another as they ran back to the field. The other team watched them quietly. Alex could tell her opponents were worried, and she was glad. Her team really did have the edge on the winning mindset, which meant they were halfway there.

Alex was so pumped. She stole the ball from Gaby, wheedled it through the players with ease, and scored. Then she scored again. And again. Because of Alex's talent and the rest of the crew's enthusiasm, they were able to take the game, and they took it fast. Neither team could even believe what had happened. The girls from 3C, with Alex in the lead, had won. But most surprising is that it hadn't even been very difficult. Alex was proud and happy and confident all at the same time.

Afterward, panting and sweating like happy puppies, the girls congratulated the other sullen-faced team, and then they hugged one another. They clapped and laughed and basked for just a few extra minutes. Even if they were getting the end-of-the-summer blues at times, everyone really had bonded over the last few weeks. They'd proven it on the soccer field—whenever someone needed support, another girl ran to her rescue. Together, when 3C needed to rally, they could do it.

Alex couldn't have been more pleased—she forgot all of her problems for that second. Nothing else mattered except that she had done her job, and she had done it well. Of course, that was typical for Alex. Anytime there were tasks to be completed, Alex was always asked to do them. Teachers knew if they needed help grading papers, Alex was their girl. Moms would let their kids stay out later as long as Alex was with them. Friends could count on Alex to help them with their homework or any other problems that they had. Alex just had this way about her of doing the right thing. But she was really hard on herself—she was a total perfectionist. Alex wasn't judgmental of others, though. She figured that people had their flaws, and those flaws made them unique, even cute. Meanwhile, she beat up on herself. She couldn't remember the last time she'd received a B in school. Anything but an A-plus was unacceptable to her. Report card day always made Alex's parents so happy—they were big on good grades.

It wasn't just school either. At camp, Alex always got up five minutes earlier than everyone else so she could tidy up her stuff after she got ready in the morning. She'd make her navy and white bed and neatly stack toiletries into her cubbyhole. Even her shoes were lined up alongside the foot of her bed. She never went frantic looking for a lost flip-flop or barrette like Brynn did. Alex never left her room—or her bunk—unless everything was in order. She was always on time (even though she was always sneaking off to take care of a secret personal errand) and during the school year, she always carried around her to-do list. Alex's mom thought Alex put too much pressure on herself. She was always giving Alex those relaxing CDs where frogs chirp and water gurgles. Alex knew she should try to take it easy, but it just didn't seem like she was built that way. She hadn't even ripped open the plastic on those calming CDs that were tucked away deep into her summer suitcase.

"It's too bad you're too young to be Color War captain," Jenna said as they headed back to the bunk to get cleaned up for dinner.

"Really? You think I'd be a good captain?" Alex asked, surprised.

"Duh!" Jenna yelled, rolling her eyes.

"But Jenna, you're really good at soccer, too," Alex said.

"I just have to admit that you're better," Jenna added. "I wish I could be captain—it would be so cool—but I was watching you out there. You've just got *it*."

Alex could feel her heart beating fast, her body getting excited. She tried not to smile too much—she didn't want to be braggy—but she almost couldn't help it. "Got what?" Alex asked.

"*It!*" Jenna and Brynn yelled at the same time.

That was a big thing for Jenna to say. She had been upset when Alex had turned out to be a better diver a few weeks ago. Alex had done everything she could to help Jenna with diving—even spent time with her at the lake—but Jenna just kept getting more and more upset when she couldn't do it right. They worked it out though, and Jenna even improved her diving. Alex understood that Jenna could be really competitive. That's why it was especially nice for her to say these things to Alex now. After all, the two of them had been coming to Camp Lakeview together forever. Even though they were close, it always felt like they were rivals albeit friendly rivals.

"Oh stop it, you all," Alex said, hoping that she really would get to be the captain in a few years. She couldn't help but think about how she'd missed being captain of her school soccer team last year.

"You're going to give Alex a big head!" Brynn interrupted, teasing her.

"Nah, we won't," Valerie added, smiling.

"Doesn't that distinction go to Chelsea anyway?" Grace whispered to Alex.

"Can we stop talking about it, please?" Alex asked, embarrassed by all the attention. She hoped they all meant it—she was thrilled! *Do they think I'm the best at sports?*

she wondered, smiling.

"Um, okay then," Karen said, and everyone hushed to look at her. Karen rarely spoke out loud. She could only be seen whispering to Chelsea, although lately she'd been standing up for herself more and not letting Chelsea boss her around *quite* so much. "I have a question for Alex. Could you tell me, what's Color War?" Karen said. Alex liked Karen a lot, even though the girl was a different kind of person. She had about twenty stuffed animals around her bed. Alex understood that girls still liked their stuffies—but everyone else had only brought one, if that.

"You've got to be kidding me," Chelsea answered, irritation in her voice. She hated when someone else got all the attention.

Alex sidled up to Karen and started telling her all about it—Color War was absolutely Alex's favorite time at camp. "That's when everyone here gets divided up into two groups, red and blue. And for three whole days, we compete with each other—even with the girls in our own bunk—to see which team will win the Lakeview Champion Title," Alex explained as her heart started beating faster.

"Um, cool," Karen said. Karen wasn't very competitive, so Alex wondered if she really meant it. But at least Karen seemed genuinely interested.

"Most of the competitions are sports," Alex said, "but not all of them. I mean, we do soccer, blob tag, Scrabble, basketball, canoeing, croquet, swimming, and singdown."

Karen's eyes lit up. Alex remembered how well Karen had sung in drama class during the first two weeks at camp. Everyone had been so shocked. This girl, who was quiet and actually kind of babyish, had an amazing, deep, grown-up voice. It was the weirdest thing Alex had seen. She hoped Karen would sing again before camp was over.

"Cool," Karen said again in a deadpan voice. Alex thought she'd be excited—she never quite understood her.

"For the first time all summer, bunkmates could be on separate teams, and best friends could be enemies," Alex added. Lucky for Alex, though, she had always managed to be on the same team as Brynn. She couldn't imagine trying to beat out her best friend in anything.

To Alex, Color War was special because while it tore the camp apart for three days, it also brought everyone closer together at the end. Unlike other camps, at Lakeview, the winners had to do something really nice for the losers—this year, like last, they would have to make chocolate chip cookies. That was always fun because those who make the cookies also get some of the dough, of course. Alex had enjoyed the process and the camaraderie and delivering the treats to the other kids at the end of dinner the year before. She hoped it would be just as much fun this year, even though she definitely wouldn't be having any treats.

The losers also had to do something for the winners. This year, each losing team in each division would have to write a poem of concession to the winners. Their poems would be read before the cookies were given out. The catch was, the poem had to be really, really funny, and it had to address why the team believed they had lost. CITs got to approve the poems or make teams go back and redo them. That night would be a really fun night, and Alex couldn't wait for it. Of course, it would be an even better night if her team won the war, but either way, it would be awesome.

Getting ready for Color War was just as much fun as actually doing it, too. The teams always got together in secret huddles to pick outfits, mascots, and cheers and to make signs and to plan pranks on their opponents. Even though Alex knew the drill by now—she still totally loved Color War at Camp Lakeview.

Last year, Alex, Sarah, and Brynn had been on the winning team together. Because they understood one another so well, they were able to score the last point for their team during a layup competition on the basketball court. After a perfect pass from Sarah, Alex threw the ball into the basket while Brynn cheered them on. They were so happy to win for their division that Alex cried a little while everyone yelled and screamed her name. She was sweaty and hugging her best friends, so she didn't think anyone had noticed how emotional she'd been.

It was a special day and a very lucky shot. She went home savoring her victory. She thought last year was the best time she'd ever had away at camp. She didn't think it could get any better.

"You're going to love it," Alex told Karen, who was a first-year. "I hope we get to be on the same team. I'll show you the secrets to winning all the different events."

Karen was so quiet that Alex hadn't gotten to know her very well. She really did hope that the two of them could hang out some more before it was time to pack up and head home in less than two weeks. But Karen was always with Chelsea, though she had been branching out after the incident at the water park. Alex was so glad that Karen wasn't letting Chelsea be so pushy anymore.

"Alex, you don't have to know everything about *everything*," Chelsea said, taking Karen aside to explain

Color War to her all over again. Alex got tingly because she could sense Karen's suffering, and she *so* wanted Karen to tell Chelsea off. Alex kind of understood, though. Sometimes, like just now, Alex didn't speak up either. Alex had the guts, that wasn't the problem, she just didn't like all the drama that came along with speaking up.

"I, um, was just answering Karen's questions," Alex said, moving away from Chelsea and over to Brynn. Brynn would tell the queen bee where to go if it became necessary. That was one thing about Brynn: No one intimidated her, and she was known to mouth off if someone pushed her buttons.

"You were showing off, Alex," Chelsea added, "and you know it. Karen, don't listen to her. I'll explain it all to you."

"I heard her, Chelsea—" Karen started to say.

Chelsea started in, "Well, it was pretty stupid to not know what Color War is. I mean, come on. Second, I would've told you, honey, if you'd just asked."

Karen hung her head down toward her feet. She was such an abused puppy most of the time, though she was slowly starting to show some teeth. Alex wondered how Karen got to be so mousy.

"I can't believe you," Brynn said to Chelsea.

Karen's eyes got white, and her face turned red. She put her head back up, and she said, "It's okay, really. I get it now, and there's no reason to—"

"Sweetie, don't you have lines to read or something? I'm sure Alex can help you learn them since she's so good at everything all the time," Chelsea added, pulling Karen ahead of the group so they would be able to jump into the showers first.

"She needs to take a chill pill," Grace said.

"She should really try meditation," Alyssa added, which came out of nowhere. Alyssa often came out of nowhere, but at least she always had something new—and unique—to say.

"Forget about her, you guys," Valerie said, walking arm-in-arm with her best friend Sarah.

"Yeah, we just won an awesome soccer game," Alex said, not wanting anyone to argue. "So let's just think about that right now."

Natalie and Alyssa ran past Chelsea and Karen, their way of beating Chelsea to the showers. Everyone was really pulling together, even Karen. It made Alex feel good.

Read more in...

camp CONFIDENTIAL

Alex's Challenge

available now!